Dragon Protectors

Slayers & Protectors Series, Book Three

This is a reverse harem urban fantasy - paranormal romance series
appropriate for ages 16+.
Mild language/swearing, open mouth kissing, low burn behind
closed-door sex scenes,
while the 17yo main character is dating four guys.
If you want to ease yourself into reverse harem, find out what the
hype is all about, then this Dragon's Story series is right for you!

USA Today Bestselling Author
Kristin D. Van Risseghem

Kasian Publishing LLC
11923 NE Sumner St, STE 759356
Portland, OR 97220
www.KristinVanRisseghem.com

Edited by
Rebecca Jaycox

Cover design by Rebecca Norinne
Irish Ink Cover Design

Author photograph by Jessica Krueger Photography

Other works by
Kristin D. Van Risseghem:

Dragon Slayer Series:
Dragon Magic, Prequel
Dragon Slayers, Book One
Dragon Wars, Book Two
Dragon Protectors, Book Three

Enlighten Series:
Swords & Stilettos, Book One
Daggers & Dresses, Book Two
Wars & Wings, Book Three

Enlighten Series Novellas:
Fires & Fairies, Sidelle's Story
Arrows & Angels, Kieran's Story

Enlighten Series Short Stories:
Poisons & Princes, Finn's Story
Ninjas & Nephilims, Shay's Story

Sign up to the Six Queens's Roundtable
Newsletter and get a FREE
exclusive set of short stories.
Go to: www.KristinVanRisseghem.com

Brooklyn is fleeing York Academy.

Blamed for the deaths of fallen slayers, Brooklyn has been labeled a traitor. People she once considered her friends are now hunting her, and the death of the city's Pride Leader has left her picking up the pieces. Brooklyn is neither ready nor prepared to become the new chief of dragons.

Until the worst happens.

One of her Protectors is being held hostage— and if Brooklyn doesn't comply with the kidnapper's demands, she might lose him forever.

Brooklyn needs more training. She needs a mentor. She needs more time.

But time is running out, for both Brooklyn and her Protectors.

Love might not be enough to save them this time.

🔥 🔥 🔥

The third book in the Slayers & Protectors series, Dragon Protectors is a reverse harem paranormal romance featuring a strong heroine trying to save her boys and prevent an all-out war. Find out what everyone's been talking about and become immersed in this magical fantasy readers call suspenseful and addicting.

Appropriate for ages 16+.

🔥 🔥 🔥

Chapter One

I'm a *what* now? I thought someone said that I'm the new Pride Leader.

The voices in my head confirm everything my four boys said to me before I went into the Slayers Council meeting.

And speaking of which, all went more than okay during the gathering. My pleas were heard, and they acquiesced to my demands. The bloodshed will end; they granted the dragons land to live on while in human form. Something isn't right, though. That was way too easy. Best be on our toes for the other shoe to drop.

I walk in a daze from the Administration building. My parents and Mr. Lorimer follow behind. I'm sure there will be more meetings in the coming weeks, hashing out exactly which islands the dragons will live on. Maybe I won't need to be part of those discussions. But then again, the leaders of the Dragon Council wouldn't want to show their human faces. I didn't want to either, but I hadn't even tried getting out of it. In fact, it was me who said that I'd go. A part of me regrets outing myself, but what's done is done.

Because I'm a dragon, my parents now understand why I'm an ex-dragon slayer. I revealed my true form to them right before we went into the Slayers meeting. If I hadn't, my folks would be slaughtering my own kin. They would be gunning for the likes of me—their own daughter.

I raise my hand to wave them off, trying to silence the chattering in my mind. It's not like the voices can see me waving at them to stop.

Mom steps to my side. "Are you okay?" she asks. "You don't look well."

"Yeah, I'm fine. I just need to rest. Today's been an emotional day with the funeral this morning, the battle, and then the council meeting." I sigh. "I'm exhausted."

"Are you coming home?" Dad asks.

"Why?"

"You just outed yourself to the Slayers Council," Mr. Lorimer says. "I don't think they'll welcome you back as a student."

"Oh. I guess I didn't think of that." What am I going to do now? I don't want to leave after I found myself. Noelle needs me as much as I need her. She's going to be grumpy about it. Plus, my boys are staying here at York. Oh, boroughs.

"You're always welcome at the penthouse, honey,"

Mom says. "It'll be just like old times, before Slayer School."

Yes, but so much as changed. I've changed—literally into a dragon. I need to see this transfer of land through. Mr. Astor was the only one who voiced his disagreement. He is the head of the Slayers School and his hatred of the dragons could be why. Maybe there were others, too, who were scared to vote against the majority. What sway does he have alone? My parents are the highest-ranking members, and many of the council members follow their lead. Does that mean they'll side with my parents, even though they don't have a daughter to protect? And if they don't, what then? A coup?

As we walk across the campus lawn, up ahead my boys are coming to meet us. The courtyard has been cleaned up as best as it could be in such a short time. At least all the bodies have been moved, and the bloodstains on the sidewalks washed away. I don't have to look at my fallen comrades and remember how they died. I want to remember their smiles and their young lives. Celebrate life. As for the exterior buildings' damage, that's still a work in progress. Stones can be replaced. People cannot be. Not a day will pass when I won't recall this day.

"How did the meeting go?" Manny asks. Like always, he's dressed in dark jeans and a shirt rolled to the elbows. He's my sweet, home-town boy.

"Hi, guys." I wave. Should I hug Manny and Bronx in front of my parents? I know Staten wouldn't want me to show my affection in front of others. My folks only know I'm dating Manny. Am I even dating Staten? "Mom, Dad, you remember Manny? He and his parents were at the same restaurant I had my birthday dinner at." I point to the other three guys. "And this is Bronx, and Staten, and McQueen. Staten is my magic instructor."

"Hello," Dad says as he shakes all their hands. "I hope Brooklyn has been a superb student for all of you."

"She has," Staten says. "Took a bit to figure out how she learns best, but eventually we got it. We need to continue her sessions, though."

"Brooklyn," John says. "You'll need to start packing your things tonight."

The boys blanch. "Why is that?" Bronx asks. "I thought the meeting went well."

"It did," I say. "They agreed to give us land."

"But," John says, "Allister is none too happy about it, and I'd hate to see Brooklyn caught in the crossfire when things go to shit."

"Are you thinking he'll back out of the deal?" Staten asks.

John shakes his head. "I don't think so. Everyone except Allister agreed on the truce, but a few of the Council members weren't there. He does have some friends. I'd just hate to have Brooklyn be at the end of his anger. That's all."

"I agree, John," Dad says as he turns to me. "You'll move back home."

I deflate. How can an eighteen-year-old move back home with her parents while dating multiple guys? What would they say about that? It's not like they said I couldn't go out nor date. I never had a curfew. I think it's just going to be different. And besides, I don't want to have my parents receive any backlash if Mr. Astor does renege on our deal.

"I'll think about it tonight and my options," I say. "But I will pack some of my belongings when I get back to my room in case I have to leave in a hurry. I have to tell Noelle if I decide to leave the school. She deserves to hear it from me in person."

"I wish you would reconsider moving home," Mom says. "But you're an adult now, and it's your choice. If you think you should stay at school, be careful. Our home is always open to you. We may not like your decision, but we'll respect it."

"I'll send your security team in the morning," Dad says.

"Thanks." I hug both my parents and then do an awkward dance with Mr. Lorimer. They veer off, heading back to their suite, while the boys and I make our way to my dorm.

The events from the meeting weigh heavily on my body

and mind. I can't help but feel that Mr. Lorimer is right. Something is coming, and we have to be ready. The Council agreed too fast in giving me everything I asked for.

I'm a dragon, and not just any dragon, but their leader.

Chapter Two

"Tell us what really happened during the meeting," Staten says as he leans against the wall. McQueen takes the chair while I sit on my bed, Manny and Bronx next to me.

They wait, and for a long time, I don't speak. I'm still trying to wrap my brain around it all. What it means for the dragons and for me. If tonight is my last night at York Academy, I want to be surrounded by my friends. My boys. And think about what's next for us. How do we move on from here?

"It went fine," I finally say.

Then I tell them how I explained to Mr. Astor that I was sent on behalf of the dragons, and they will stop killing slayers if the Council would grant the land. I tell them how he tried to force magic onto me, but it didn't do anything. My parents sensed what he was doing and interceded on my behalf. A vote was called to kick my family out of the meeting because of their bias, but no one seconded the motion. Mrs. Mercer asked for assurances. She asked me if I was one of them, and without any hesitation, I confirmed it. That was when an internal blast of magic filled me, and I saw colored flames mix with mine. I thought magic was pulled from the Council members into me. But what I felt was something entirely different. My body started to change. I gained control and stopped the shift. After that, I could hear the dragons in my mind. My parents were the first to agree to giving us land, and eventually the rest of the room voted yes.

We are silent, my boys absorbing my words. I stand and find my luggage. Slowly, I pack my shoes and duster bags. I feel their eyes on me, following my movements. In the closeness within my room, not only can I hear my boys' thoughts of shock and hope, but there are others that fill my head now, too. None of the new voices are talking to each other, just voicing their internal thoughts. I don't know how I know the difference, but I do. Will I ever have a moment's quiet again?

Leaving them to their thoughts, I continue placing clothes into another bag. Then I begin gathering dresses.

"You're really leaving?" Manny asks.

I nod. "I think Mr. Lor—I mean John—is right. Tomorrow when the sun rises and Mr. Astor has time to think about what happened during the meeting, he'll want to silence me. I can't be here. Do you think he'll go after my parents directly?"

Sure, I'm scared, but they come first. I can't go home. I need to protect my family. That would put them in danger. If Mr. Astor comes for me, I won't put them in harm's way. I'll have to get word to them once I figure out where I'm going to stay while things get sorted, and Mr. Astor makes the first move—if he does.

"I don't know," Manny says. "But he won't hurt you, Brooklyn. Not while we're here to protect you. He'll have to go through us."

"Yeah, that's right, Sweetheart," Bronx says.

"We've got your back, Babe," McQueen says.

"I don't want to put a downer on that, but he could send someone to take her out," Staten says. "Or tell the students and let them do the work for him. And of course I stand with my brothers."

I smile. Of course, my boys, my protectors, would have my best interests in their hearts. Continuing folding jeans, pants, and shorts, I'm about finished emptying my room of my belongings.

"Thank you," I say. "You know I love you guys, right?"

"Yes," they say.

"I'm not going home. I can't put my folks in danger. If Allister sends someone to kill me, what's to stop him from sending someone to kill them?"

"Where are you going to live?" Bronx asks.

"Not sure yet. A hotel, maybe, until I can figure something else out." I shrug. "Maybe Dad will rent me a place."

"Nonsense." McQueen stands before me and takes my hands. "Come live with my family. You can continue training with magic and skills with me. I can show you more about dragon shifting. Plus, my dad will want to discuss things with you now that you're the Pride Leader. Or you could live where you want. Someone within the Pride will take you in. They'd be honored to have you as a guest until a more permanent solution arises."

"How did you know about me being the leader?"

"We felt the change," Staten says. "After Regan died, his power and magic transferred to you, didn't it?" I nod. "The dragons have been floundering for a bit, and Dad has stepped in to take that roll, plus his High Councilman duties. But you're now here to take back what you are meant to do. I think I speak for everyone here when I say we knew the moment you embraced your true self this evening. Our magic merged with yours, claiming you as our leader. So not only are you a part of us on a protector level, but we gave you more of ourselves when you finally acknowledged your birthright."

"I think you should go live with McQueen," Manny

says. "Any one of our folks would offer you to stay with them, but he said it first. That way, McQueen can continue working with you while we're here learning about Allister's plans, and maybe with our mental connections, we'll be able to warn you ahead of time." Everyone nods. "I'll let you finish packing and go find Noelle for you."

What am I going to say to her? I know I should tell her … and I will. Oh boroughs, she's going to freak out. And that's making me anxious. "Thank you." I stand and gently kiss his check. He's sweet to remember I wanted to say goodbye to my best friend. "Make sure you come find me in the morning before I leave."

"I will."

"Great. I'll let Dad know and prepare a room for you," McQueen says. "I'll text you my address, so just come over when you're ready. I assume the boys will help you load your car in the morning. If it doesn't all fit, we'll send for the rest."

That leaves Staten and Bronx with me tonight. Never once has Staten volunteered to watch over me, so this'll be interesting. Sure he kinda watches over me when we're asleep and he brings me into the dragon dream realm, but that's not the same thing as being physically next to me or even in the same room. Since the cabin, I find him a bit standoffish. Perhaps that's me reading into it. The closeness I have with his brothers will come with him, too.

There's no need to rush it. I know he cares for me. He doesn't always vocalize it or show it, but I know from the few tender touches he's made. I should tell and show him more, so he gets comfortable hearing it from me.

"I'll find out what Allister is thinking," Staten says. "He won't trust John anymore, and I'm the next best magic user he has." He stands by the door with his brothers.

"Staten, can I have a word with you for a moment before you guys leave?" I ask.

He nods.

"I'll be right back, Sweetheart, while you and Staten talk," Bronx says. "I'm just going to run back to my room for a change of clothes. I'll bring back snacks."

We watch the three guys go, leaving me with my tallest and oldest protector, Staten. He's his quiet self. His early monologue was the first time I've heard him say that many words.

I walk back to my bed, patting the side next to me.

"What's on your mind, Brooklyn?"

"Is there a way to block out the voices of the others?" I point to my head. "All of the dragons in our Pride are in here chatting. I can hear you guys still, too." His eyes widen. "It's not like before when you guys speak with me. It's more like I can hear your inner monologue. I didn't want to say anything while everyone else was in the room. I just thought you'd know of a way to block everything out."

"Maybe." He takes my hands with a gentleness that still surprises me. "Regan never hinted that it was a burden to him hearing everyone, so maybe he found a way to silence them until he needed to communicate with everyone. Leadership is usually passed down to the next while the current leader is still alive, so with his death, you'll have a bit of learning to do on that. I want you to try something for me. If it doesn't work, then maybe Dad can help you. Close your eyes."

"Okay." We slow our breathing.

"Focus on your magic. Let it spread over your body. Think about what you want it to do."

My body hums immediately. Since I accepted leadership of the dragons, my magic is easy to call. It has done what I want the few times I've needed it. This time isn't any different. Sending the power into my mind, I coax it to wrap around only the voices. They dampen, and eventually they become quiet.

"It's getting easier for you, isn't it?" Staten asks.

I open my eyes. "It is. Thank you for helping me with this."

"I don't think you're going to need my help anymore."

"I'll always need you, Staten."

I gaze into his hazel eyes. He leans into me. Is he going to kiss me? That would be a new dynamic to our relationship. He's only ever showed me his affections in dragon form and that one morning at my cabin, but never in front of anyone. Someone could walk by and catch us. Sometimes, I have caught him glimpsing me with longing. I bite my lip and close the distance.

His body freezes but only for a second. There isn't any doubt left in him. His soft lips brush against mine as his hand cups my head, securing me as if he doesn't want me to move. I know now that I don't want to be anywhere but here with him.

The kiss ends much too soon. I like seeing Staten like this, his barriers down. He's still a bit awkward, not knowing what to do with his hands after he removes them from my hair. His heartbeat pounds against his chest. He tilts his forehead to mine, palming my cheek. "Thank you," he says.

"For what?" My own heart thumps against my ribs.

"For allowing me to kiss you. I didn't want you going into the lion's den without one of us. I wasn't sure if you'd come out alive, but here you are. I didn't want this chance to go by without me tasting your lips. I might not ever get the chance again."

"I'm sure there is still so much you can teach me," I say, a bit breathless. He smiles, flashing me his sexy dimples. The grin he only gives to me. "You guys will have to come visit me on the weekends." I shake my head. "There won't be any more missions, right?"

"I don't know. We'll find out what the Academy is going to do next. We have funerals to plan, regroup, and sort out the remaining students. Our covers haven't been blown, so we need to stay here and be watchful and pass any information we learn to you and the Council."

He came to the same conclusion I had. We need eyes and ears inside the school.

Chapter Three

Staten leaves shortly after promising that Bronx is on his way and that he has to find out what Allister is thinking- otherwise he would've stayed with me. Then we could have that convo about the morning at the cabin. I'll just find another time to talk about that with him.

I continue packing my toiletries until Bronx knocks on the door with a bag over his shoulder. "You still packing?" he asks when he steps into my room.

"Yep, but I'm almost done."

"Here." He hands me a to-go box. "I brought you a burger and fries. I know you love them."

"Thanks!" I hadn't realized I was hungry until the smell of food wafted into my nose. "You're so good to me."

"I aim to please, Sweetheart."

I take a break from filling my suitcases and eat dinner with Bronx. We're both quiet in a comfortable way. Normally, Bronx is laughing and being a flirt, but he knows the seriousness of the situation.

"How's your food?" Bronx asks.

"It's fine. Thank you again for bringing it."

"You and McQueen?" He tilts his head.

"Do you really want to know?"

"Not really."

"My dragon seems to like him." I stuff a fry in my mouth. "How come you guys are all okay with me dating all of you?"

"If that's what you want, who are we to say that you can only be with one of us? We each have our strengths that you're drawn to, just like we are drawn to you. It's you fulfilling our needs. Yes, our openness might seem unconventional to others, or what people perceive to be the normal way of dating, but that's them and not us, or you."

"I see."

He takes my burger from my hands and places it on the tray, threading his fingers through mine. "You still have doubt in your eyes. Do you love your mom and dad?"

"Yes, of course." I nod.

"Each of them fills a role in your life. It'd be hard to choose one of them over the other because of that. Neither of them is jealous of the other when they spend time with you. What you do with your mom is different than with your dad. While I can only guess that your dad doesn't prefer taking you to spas and shopping, he would if you asked him to. But that is what you and your mom like doing together."

"Dad and I like going to the theatre together. Mom tolerates it but would rather go to the galleries."

"See, having the four of us in your life is just like that."

"I don't have sex with them, though."

"You don't have to with us either, but the concept of loving us and going into more intimate situations is going to be different with each of one of us. It's not like you'll sleep with us all at the same time. I can guess that it is a special moment for each of us, at a special place and time."

I know I've asked Manny that question before, and he gave me basically the same response. But that was before Staten and I had sex, too.

"Is Noelle going to stay with you tonight?" Bronx asks.

"I don't know. Haven't really thought about it yet. I'm not sure how she's going to take me leaving her, since we just buried Sax yesterday. I need to stay for Reist's funeral, and I'd like to be there for Lexi's, too." I can't even think about what tomorrow will bring when all the feelings I've been smashing down come to light. The guilt of their deaths by my dragons. It wasn't my hand that made the killing shots, but those dragons are my responsibility.

Sure, I just became friends with some of my Level Twoers these past few weeks, but they were still my classmates. I might not have spoken to them until this year, but we bonded over the weekend. I won't turn my back on them just because I'm fighting on the other side of the war. "But if she doesn't stay, you are, right?"

"I wouldn't have it any other way. It'll be my last chance for a while. McQueen will be the lucky bastard when you leave here."

My room now looks barren. I remember a time not so long ago when I thought about leaving the Academy and doing something else with my life. Even though my parents are on the Slayers Council and it was unspoken that I'd attend this school and become a dragon slayer, I felt something was missing. And now I know what it was.

It's not that I didn't belong here. I'm glad I came. I wouldn't have met my boys. I wouldn't have met my best friend Noelle or Reist, Sax, or my Team Magic Users. I think I was supposed to come here, learn, and understand the stakes, meeting these people along the way to reinforce my true heritage.

Seeing Sax die on the last Level Three mission solidified it in my mind, knowing that the Slayers Council had to stop killing us. But when the dragons retaliated and killed six instructors, four staff, ten visiting family members, and forty-seven of my peers, I broke.

"Hey, what's going on?" Noelle steps into my room and glances around. "Manny said that you were looking for me."

"I'll be back later, Sweetheart." Bronx kisses me on the lips and leaves us.

Oh, boroughs. How am I going to do this? She can't handle any more bad news. For the last week, she's been a zombie. Just over this weekend, she started acting like her old, bubbly self.

"Where's all your stuff?" she asks. I don't say anything. Tears swell in my eyes. "Brooklyn? Why have you packed your things?" Her voice is harsh.

"There's something I need to tell you, Noelle." I wring my hands.

"Are you preggers? You better not be. You're much too young for that."

I shake my head. "No, I'm not pregnant."

"Good. Now what's up? You better start talking and not beating around the bush. I can see that your room is empty and you're leaving. I want to know why."

Closing the door, I turn back and sit next to her on the bed. "I'm not safe here anymore. My parents took me to the Council meeting tonight, and although things went as planned, my folks don't think I should stay at the school."

"But—"

I hold up a hand. "You know why we are here at the Academy?" It's a rhetorical question, and I don't give her a chance to respond. "The dragons want peace and land to call their home. The Council decided to give in to their

20

demands after last night's battle."

"I don't see why you have to go, though. And how could the Council do that? After they killed all those people, we should be fighting back."

"Revenge won't bring Sax back. Or Reist. Or Lexi." I grab hold of Noelle's hands from her lap. "This is bigger than you and me. It's more than what anyone has ever told us. I know you want revenge for Sax's death. But I can't be part of that. I won't kill any more dragons."

"How can you say that? You're a Kill Shot."

"Not anymore."

"I don't think you can give that title back."

"True. But I don't need to take any more dragons' lives. I'm not a slayer anymore once I leave tomorrow morning."

"What aren't you telling me?"

I hadn't planned on telling Noelle this yet. I figured we had time, at least another year. She could still find her magic, and if she didn't, she could take one of the instructor positions. Now, they'll have more openings than applicants. Then I correct myself. They won't need the school since we've called a truce. Yes, there will be a transition period, but teaching weapons and tactical combat won't be needed any longer.

"You can tell me anything, Brooklyn," she says. "Whatever it is, it can't be that bad. Not any worse than dying. No one comes back from that."

I look into her eyes. They, too, are wet from tears that are forming. "Noelle." I take a deep breath and close my eyes. I can't see the betrayal, disgust, anger, or whatever other feeling she'll reveal when I say it. "I'm a dragon."

Chapter Four

The room is as silent as the dead. The only noise is the hum from the lights and our heartbeats. I don't even think Noelle is breathing.

I open my eyes. "Say something," I demand.

Her eyes scan my body up and down, looking for a sign that I'm speaking the truth. It's not that I go around in my dragon form all the time. But I think I can use a bit of magic to show her something. Bright green flames flare and slither over my hands. I focus on them, and the skin shimmers like waves, and green scales morph across my flesh.

Noelle's eyes bulge, and she shakes her head. My gaze seeks hers. She's not scared of me but surprised. "For reals?" she asks. I nod as I bite my lip. She needs to talk, so I know she can accept me for who I am. "Get out!" Her voice rises as a tiny smile plays on her lips. "How long have you known?"

"Not a long time."

"Like yesterday? Last month? Five years ago? How in the world are you a dragon? If you are ... then your boys ... How could you keep that from me? I'm your BFF. We're supposed to share. That means everything. You don't keep something like that to yourself. Gosh, that must have been hard for you."

"Slow down, Noelle." She's firing off more questions than I can answer. "I've known for a couple of weeks. But I can't tell you anything else, so please don't ask."

"So a full-on dragon." She nods. "Cool."

"I'm sorry for not telling you. It's just that I just found out myself and have been wrapping my brain around that. Learning new skills and being worried about what you'd say and how you'd take the news. It's not every day someone tells you that they're a dragon."

"True. But promise you won't keeping things of this magnitude from me ever again."

"I promise." I smile. "So, cool? That's what you're going to go with?"

"What do you want me to say? You are who you are. No magic in the world, especially mine since I don't have any, will change that." She looks at our locked hands. "Can do you that again? I want to see it." I show her my scales again, forming my hand into a claw. Her body tenses for a second and then relaxes. "You breathe fire, right?" I nod. "Someday, you're going to show me your full form."

"You're not scared?"

"Of you?" She waves her hand. "Naw, you wouldn't hurt a fly, especially your friends. I honestly didn't think you had it in you to be a Kill Shot. That surprised all of us. Everyone was betting that Reist would be it." There is a pause in the room when she says our fallen classmate's name. He won't ever be anything again. "Who was that new guy I've seen hanging around your boys?" Noelle asks. "You know, the one who drove us to … I didn't get a chance to ask before … you know, the burial ceremony. He's pretty bad-ass looking. And no, you're not off the hook yet for the dragon thing."

"He's arrogant and selfish. Stay away from him." I swat her arm. "He's trouble and knows it. McQueen is their brother-in-arms."

"So right up your alley, then?"

"No way. I've got my hands full already."

"So you don't want to do the nasty with McHottie?"

I blush, remembering the sizzling kiss he stole when we first met in the woods. Then how his body pressed against mine when he taught me to play pool.

"I'll take your non-response as a yes." Noelle winks.

"It's not like that."

"Sure it isn't." She smiles. "Where are you really

going?"

"I'm staying with McQueen until things gets sorted out."

"So while you're staying with him at his house for who knows how long, no shenanigans will be had? Zero? None? Zilch?"

"No. He's training me in magic, Skills, and in my dragon form. It's strictly professional." I have no idea why I'm even saying this to her. She knows it's a lie. Purring rumbles from my chest.

"What is that?"

"It's nothing." My face flushes.

"It's so not nothing." She pokes her hand at me. "You like him. Like, *like* him. And if you don't, your dragon does. Right?"

I sigh. "Yes. She's smitten with him."

"Isn't she you?"

"Yes, in a way. It's hard to explain."

"So if your dragon likes McQueen … he's a dragon, too?"

I press my lips together. I won't out them, even to my best friend. It's not my secret to share. If they want her to know, they can tell her. "I can't confirm that."

"That's okay; you don't have to. I already know the answer. Makes sense if you ask me. Why they are all enamored with you, and you with them. I've told you once it doesn't matter what others think. You go and date all those hotties and take them off the market. They clearly only have eyes for you."

"You're going to be okay without me for a while?"

"Sure. Your boy toys will keep me company. They might not warm my bed, but they'll let me know how you're doing. Plus, you'll still have a phone, and you can call me. Maybe over the weekends I can come visit you at McQueen's place or something." Noelle stands and starts handing me a couple of random items off my dresser. "They are staying here, right? They're not going with you?"

"No, they are staying."

"Okay." She picks up one of the blue jewelry boxes. "Don't forget to pack these. You should put them in your purse so you don't lose them."

"Thanks." I place all three boxes into my purse. She's right, of course; I wouldn't want to lose any of it. Each piece is special, given to me by my boys. Manny gave me the dragon necklace, Bronx gave me the ring, and Staten the earrings for my birthday gifts. The dragons have green emeralds for eyes, diamonds along the wings, and then a unique design. "Noelle? I can trust you, right? I mean I've told you a ton of information that you could take right back to the Slayers Council and destroy the dragons with."

"I'm shocked you even have to ask. But I understand.

You're looking out for yourself, your boys, and the dragons. I guess I would, too. Yes, Brooklyn, you can trust me with this." She glances around the dorm. "Looks like you're about done. What time are you leaving tomorrow?"

"Sometime in the morning. We'll load my car, and I'll either come back for anything else or have it delivered to McQueen's house."

"If you're not safe here, should you be announcing where the luggage should go?"

"You're right. I should just leave everything and buy new." Boroughs, why didn't I think about that?

I snag my cell phone off the bed and text McQueen.

Me: You coming over in the morning? I think you should and take what I can't fit in my car. Noelle says that no one from school will know where to find me.

If he brings his car, all my stuff should fit in both of our vehicles.

McQueen: Sure. Text me the time when you've figured that out. See you in the morning, Babe.

"Let's do breakfast tomorrow, and then you can leave?" Noelle asks.

"Sure, it's date."

We hug for a long time. It's not weird at all, and I mean it. Last year, this would have been awkward for me. I didn't have any friends then, and to let myself feel vulnerable or emotional would never have happened. I'll miss seeing Noelle every day, but like she said, she is only a phone call away. And I know McQueen lives someplace in the city, so we can always meet someplace, or she can come over.

This isn't goodbye.

Chapter Five

Noelle decides to leave. If tonight is my last night and my boys are staying here, then she knows they would like to spend the night with me. And she knows I want that, too. I'm not alone for long. Bronx swaggers back into my room as I ready for bed. My bags sit near the door, waiting to be brought up to the lobby in the morning. I left my satchel with my laptop and purse with my most treasured items on the built-in desk. Those are the only things I'll be carrying with me when I leave.

I climb into bed, and Bronx sits next to me. The room is quiet, except for our breathing.

I remember that very first day when I met Manny, my personal tour guide at the Academy. He was so sweet, and I was a dork who stared at him. He never said anything about my awkwardness or being spacey because I was staring at his hot body.

Manny was my very first boyfriend. The first guy I kissed, and the first man I slept with. This school would hold great memories of him, of us, for me.

Then there is Bronx, the flirty guy who waltzed into my life shortly after Manny and I became a couple. He made me laugh with his corny one-liners. Still does.

Then there is the oldest and quietest one of the bunch, Staten. He, too, will have a special place in my memories of school. We didn't start off the best. In fact, there are times he still gives me harsh looks or clipped words. But I understand him probably the best, even though we don't talk or hang out as much as I do with his brothers. We get each other on a deeper level. It just took us longer to get where we are today.

And lastly there is McQueen. The naked boy I saw in the park while his brothers tried helping him with a stab wound. His swagger and confidence come off sometimes as dickish, but he knows who he is inside and out. He's the most loyal of the four boys, the fiercest, and the most reckless one, too.

Yes, I will miss being here.

"What are you thinking about?" Bronx's deep voice breaks the silence.

"You, actually." I squeeze his hand.

"And what about me?"

"Your hot body." He can't see me smiling. "Your strong

arms, broad chest ... the way you flirt with me." I run a finger up his arm.

He shivers. "And what do you want to do about that?"

"Nothing." I turn to face him, grinning. "You asked what I was thinking, and I told you. Actually, though, I was thinking of all your brothers, not just you."

"I think I need a cold shower."

I laugh. "Tonight is my last night here, and I was thinking how each of you came into my life. If I hadn't been here, where would we be? Would we have still met? Now, I can't imagine my life without any one of you. Each of you is dear to me."

"You are to us, too." He adjusts his body, leaning on his hand. "I don't think I've ever told you this but before I met you, my life was empty. I sought companionship with lots of girls."

"Yeah, I don't think I need to hear about your sexual adventures with—"

He halts my words with a kiss. "That's not where I was going. I spent time with a lot of girls, but they were never enough. I went through them almost weekly."

"Not helping, Bronx."

He grins. "Stop interrupting me. All those girls never filled the part of me that I didn't realize was missing until I met you. Brooklyn, you fill that vacant piece to my soul. You make me whole. You make me a better man, the one

I'm meant to be. Since you came into my life, there has been no other girl I've wanted to date, kiss, or be with more than you. You've captured my heart, body, and mind. I can only offer you this." He places my hand over his beating heart. "I've told you that I love you, and I do, but I want to give you something more. Something that I've wanted you to have for a long time. I just didn't know when the right time was, but I think it's now."

What more could he possibly give me?

The air shimmers, and Bronx calls forth his magic. A blue tint fills the room. My bright green flames greet his. It bends, swirling light on the bed covers. The magic dances, but it's always separate, a thin line between them.

Rumbles emit from Bronx's chest. The skin over his torso changes into green scales, and slowly his neck morphs into that of a dragon, then his nose elongates to form a snout. His teeth lower from the gum line as his mouth opens, and a fireball hovers in the air. His right hand, which did not turn into a claw, reaches up and grabs the spark. Everything that was part dragon is now fully human again. The reddish-orange flame hangs suspended above his palm. His blue magic retreats and absorbs into the fireball.

"What's happening?" I ask.

"Just wait. It's almost done. Once this is complete, I can't offer this to anyone else. It's permanent."

Emerald green flashes, wrapping around the magic and then floats back to me. Tapping warm sparks along my entire body, the flame moves back to my chest and sinks into me. I can feel the heat around my heart, lungs, and then it zips into my bloodstream.

Fingers thread through mine. Lips press lightly on my forehead, cheeks, and finally my lips. His tongue coaxes my mouth open. I let him in.

"Brooklyn."

"Yes, Bronx?"

"How do you feel?"

How do I feel? Not only do I feel warm and tingly, I feel him. Not only in my fingers and lips but everywhere. I peel away from him, opening my eyes. We are not touching except for our hands. "I can feel you as if you are actually touching my body." I blink. "It's like you're in my head. Not only with your voice, but with something more. There's an ache in my heart that I don't think is mine. Is that coming from you?"

"Yes. Not only can you now hear me, but you can feel what I'm feeling and thinking. It's stronger than the magic bond you have with Staten. What I shared with you is part of my dragon. You and your dragon have accepted me as yours. I told you I gave you my heart, and this is my dragon giving you his soul. Neither I nor my dragon can live without you. If you die, so do I."

What?

"I can't—"

He presses a finger against my lips. "It's not something I can take back. It's yours now. I am yours, always and forever. You will know when I'm in distress, sleeping, and so much more. It's the ultimate gift a dragon can give. I know I should have told you before I did it, but I didn't want there to be a chance that you wouldn't accept it. Besides, some part of you had to have known, otherwise it wouldn't have worked. Your magic, dragon, or you wouldn't have allowed the merge."

"Bronx." I place a gentle kiss on his lips. "Thank you."

He rises from the bed. "You're not staying?"

"No. We've got too much stuff to do early in the morning. I wish I could, Sweetheart. God, do I want to stay and have you spend your last night in my arms. I don't know when we'll next have a chance." He brushes another kiss on my lips, pulling away. I can see the torment in his eyes. He doesn't want to leave. I don't want him to leave. "I need to go before I end up staying." With another chaste kiss, he runs his fingers through his hair and departs.

I'm shrouded in darkness and silence. My body relaxes as I think about what just happened between Bronx and me. He gave me a part of his soul. Holy boroughs. I'll forever have him with me. Do I want to hear all his thoughts? I definitely don't need him hearing mine all the time. It's bad enough having the Pride in my mind.

I guess we'll see what happens and how it works exactly. My body knows he's gone. There's a dull ache in my chest. I felt it the minute he left. He's not in my mind, or if he is, he's quiet. Closing my eyes, I let out a deep breath. Do the others want to follow what Bronx did? I can't be responsible for their lives. They are dragons, so in a way, I guess I am. But this is taking it well past the finishing line.

"Brooklyn?" Manny's voice is in my mind. *"Are you awake? Stop whatever it is you're doing and get out. Leave, lock the door, and go. I know Bronx just left you. He's on his way back, but we think it's better if you do this before he gets there. Things could get messy and …"*

"What's wrong?" I ask. *"I don't understand."* From his urgent voice, I know something is not right. Quickly dressing, I lace my sneakers and strap my purse and satchel across my body. *"Manny?"* I ask. *"What are you not telling us?"*

"You need to get to the garage and drive to McQueen's place immediately." I open the door, checking down the hall. I can barely get the door locked. *"A mob is coming for you, Brooklyn,"* Manny continues. *"Someone overheard Allister talking about the meeting and what was agreed to. People don't like it that the humans are standing down and not fighting back to avenge their fallen."*

That gets me going. I run out of the building. Digging into my purse, I fumble for my keys. There are angry shouts, and a large group of kids walk toward the girl's dorm. When they spot me, they run.

I make it into the parking garage, my satchel bouncing against my side. The black convertible is where I left it. A beep alerts me that the doors are unlocked. I climb into the driver's seat and strap myself in as the engine starts, peeling out of the parking spot.

The tires squeal, turning fast and leaving smoke in their wake. Glancing out of the passenger side window, there are about twenty staff members pouring into the garage entrance. I do not slow down. Everyone scatters, leaping out of the way as my vehicle heads right for them.

The only saving grace is that I managed to get away before anyone was physically hurt, but now they must know someone is helping me. They'll know maybe it's Manny or Bronx. I don't think they'll assume it was Staten.

It's going to make my boys a target.

Chapter Six

I cruise aimlessly around the city, doubling back and watching the rearview mirror. The streets bustle with cars and people, even at this time of night. New York is the city that never sleeps. I drive a couple of blocks from the Academy until I know there is no one following me, which isn't likely since most students don't have vehicles at the school.

Pulling over, I find a parking spot and calm my breathing. My white knuckles grip the steering wheel. I force myself to unclench them. Letting out a sigh, I dig into my purse for my phone. Pressing on the screen, I send a text to McQueen, hoping he's up and that the boys have told him what happened.

Me: Are you awake?

My phone vibrates with an incoming text.

McQueen: What's up, Babe?
Me: I'm on my way to your house right now.
McQueen: Why? What's wrong?
Me: Send me your address, and we'll talk when I arrive. Too much to text.
McQueen: 710 Point Crescent, Queens

I bring Google Maps up as I navigate to his house. Once I'm out of the city, I cruise along into the Soundview neighborhoods and then over the Whitestone Bridge into the Malba area of homes.

Finding the correct residence after Center Drive turns into Point Crescent, I see large single-family homes towering in the streetlights. Tall trees hide the driveway as I zoom past it and have to turn back around. A gate blocks the entrance. Creeping up to the black box, I press the button to announce my arrival.

"Hello?" I say. "I'm here to see McQueen." It sounds corny, but I don't know his first name. No one has ever told it to me and I never asked.

"Hi, Babe. Just drive up and leave your car near the fountain." The gate swings open, allowing me to enter.

Fountain?

Yup, a few feet in front of me sits a ten-foot water

fountain. Just past that is a staircase leading to the front door. Lights spill from the house, and I can see that it's two stories with white trim and coral-colored stucco siding. Tan marble steps set off the residence. This is not the house I would've pictured McQueen living in. I leave my car where he suggested as I make my way up the stairs.

McQueen stands in the entrance, holding the door open. "Are you all right?" he asks.

"Yeah. I'm sorry it's so late. I—"

He brings me into a tight hug. "Manny called me right after you texted and filled me in. They'll try to grab your stuff and bring it here, but it might be a couple of days."

"That's okay. I can go home tomorrow for clothes if you think it'll be safe."

"Come on in, and let's get you settled." He flips off the exterior lights, motioning me to follow him.

As we move through the house, I get a glimpse of the rooms. Everything is white marble. It reminds me of the houses in Italy. We head to the lower level, and a lemongrass fragrance fills my nostrils. I know we're close to his room.

I'm not staying in his bedroom this whole time, am I?

"Tomorrow, I'll give you the grand tour. It's probably not as posh as your pad, but it's a roof over our heads."

Actually, it is pretty swanky and in a nice neighborhood. If my parents wanted a house in the city, we'd probably live in something like this. But no one has the great views we have in our high rise.

"Since you had to leave so quickly, you can borrow a shirt of mine to sleep in."

"Um, and where will that be exactly?" I look around his room. It's large and messy, things just dropped on the floor or scattered across surfaces. My fingers itch to straighten the clothes peeking out from the dresser drawers that are left half open. "I don't know how long I'll be staying, and I don't want to intrude any more than I have to, but I can't stay in your room."

"As much as I'd love for you to stay in here, I have made arrangements for your own space." A smile stretches across his face. "You don't have anything to unpack, so why be in there by yourself?" He yanks open the closet door and hands me a clean shirt.

I'm going to drown in it, but it's better than nothing. "Thanks." It smells like him: lemongrass.

He walks through a door and comes back out with a toothbrush, paste, and a little blue familiar box. "Here." I take the newly wrapped brush and the trial size toothpaste. Holding them tight against my body, these are the only things I can call my own. For now. The box still lays in my hand. I stare at it.

"Oh, here." He clears off a spot for me on his king-sized bed. "Sit if you'd like. I was told it was your birthday last week."

I sit and glance around his room again. The cream-colored walls are plastered with posters and pictures of cars, trucks, and motorcycles. My purse and bag straps fall off my shoulders. I finally relax a bit. "Yeah, I turned eighteen."

"I know."

I glance back at the box. "What is it? You didn't have to get me anything."

"I know I didn't, but I wanted to. Open it and find out."

Slowly, I lift the lid. A dragon bracelet nestles in between the silk pillows. The emerald eyes sparkle at me while the diamonds around the spine accent nicely against the silver metal. It matches the rest of my jewelry.

"I love it, McQueen. Thank you."

"You're welcome. You look exhausted, Babe. Do you want to go to sleep?"

"I am tired, but I can stay up for a while longer."

"I'm not doing anything important. You're going to fall over soon. Why don't you go to bed, and we can chat in the morning?" He holds out his hand to me. "Come on. I'll show you to your room."

Standing, I grab my meager belongings and take McQueen's warm hand. He leads us out of his bedroom and down a hall. Opening the door, he lets me pass and then flips on the light.

The room is identical to his but smaller. The same flooring, the same color on the walls, the same layout, but this space is neat and tidy.

I lay the shirt and toiletries on the dresser beside my purse and satchel.

McQueen brushes past me, opening another door. "Your private bathroom is here. I'll, um, leave you to it then. Have a good night, Babe." He walks to the door.

"McQueen?"

"Yeah?" He turns to face me. "Did you need something?"

"No. It's just … What's your first name?"

"No one calls me it."

"Oh." I look at my shoes. I should've removed them when I entered the house.

He blows out a sigh. "Macklin."

I tilt my head and walk toward him. "Really?" I ask softly as I lower his head down, so I can look into his jade eyes.

"Yep. Macklin Queen. It's why everyone calls me McQueen."

"So, Queen is your last name?"

"It is."

"It's nice. You're first name, I mean." Standing on my tiptoes, I kiss his cheek. "You should use it more. I like it."

He shakes his head, leaving me for the night.

Chapter Seven

I wake after a short, restless slumber. My dreams were a tangled mess of dragons, kids chasing me, and blood. So much blood and death. I lean forward, bringing my knees to my chest. The room, although still bathed in darkness, is warm. Inhaling McQueen's lemongrass scent from his shirt soothes my addled brain.

A shadow passes under the doorway. I think it's McQueen standing outside my room. Will he knock or just come in? After a few moments of silence, the door remains closed. The pattering of feet fades. I lie back down on the soft bed and shut my eyes.

When I wake again, sunlight streams into the room, making lines across the floor from the wooden blinds. Today, I need to let my parents know that I left school. They don't need to know where I'm staying. They don't need trouble brought to their front door. If the students and staff retaliate against me, then the Council might do the same to them.

I brush my teeth and run fingers through my hair. Stepping out of the room, I glance down, and sitting on the floor is a T-shirt and yoga pants. Holding the bottoms up, I judge they should fit. Are they from McQueen's mom? The shirt is still his own. Returning to the room, I quickly change into the new clothes.

When I exit, McQueen is leaning against the doorframe. "I see you got my gift." His eyes scan my body.

"Yeah, thanks again."

"Anytime. How did you sleep?"

"Okay, all things considered."

He nods, holding out a hand. "Come, let's go get some breakfast." He kisses my forehead. "Then you can meet my folks. My dad is especially interested in meeting you."

I stop dead in my tracks, glancing down at my attire.

"Don't worry about it. You're fine. In fact, he won't be in a power suit or anything."

It doesn't help. I shouldn't be meeting the head of the Dragon Council in a T-shirt and yoga pants. I wiggle my toes. And in bare feet. But if McQueen says it'll be okay, then it will be. His dad has to understand the circumstances of last night.

We walk into a grand kitchen. Even in here, everything is white and reminds me of my own kitchen at home. McQueen walks to the fridge and holds out the milk and orange juice. "What kind of cereal do you like?" He goes and grabs bowls and spoons.

I sit on a barstool and shrug. "I don't know; what do you have?" He steps aside to allow me a view of the pantry. Lining the shelf is every cereal box imaginable: sweet ones like Coco Pebbles and healthy ones like Raisin Bran. I smile when I see the orange box. "Peanut Butter Captain Crunch, please."

McQueen removes the box from the shelf and hands me it so I can pour in the amount I want. I haven't had this since I was a little girl.

"Do you want coffee?" he asks. "I don't drink it, but I think I might be able to figure out how to turn the blasted machine on."

"Naw, that's okay. I'll just have the leftover milk in the cereal." I spoon in a mouthful of breakfast. "Thanks for letting me stay here."

He only nods, crunching away with his mixed bowl of Cheerios and Kashi Puffs.

I glance at the clock on the stove. It's just past eight in the morning, a bit too early to call my parents. "Are you coming with me today when I go to the penthouse?"

"Yes," McQueen says. "And we'll take one of our vehicles." I tilt my head in question. "So others don't recognize you, and we'll fit more into the trunk than you could in your convertible."

Yeah, he's right about that. We continue eating breakfast in silence, watching each other as more sunlight pours in through the glass doors leading into the backyard. Once I'm done with my bowl, I rinse it out and lay it in the sink.

My feet take me to sliding glass doors, overlooking the view in the yard. It's large, even with the fenced area for the in-ground pool. A high retaining wall shields the property from prying neighbors. Farther past their property line is the East River. The scenery is spectacular. I bet I could see all the way across on a clear day.

"This is Powell Cove." McQueen stands next to me.

"It's beautiful."

"Yeah." He scans my body. "It's even better now that you're here."

I blush. Last night, McQueen wasn't his normal, sure self. He was quiet and melancholy. But this morning, he's back to his swaggering ways. I'm so lost in my thoughts I don't hear others in the kitchen. I'm surprised when I turn around.

A gorgeous, blond-haired woman is waiting for the coffee machine. Now, I know where McQueen gets his blond hair. Her long, manicured nails tap the white countertop. She's thin, but not too skinny. Her back is held perfectly straight. "Oh, good morning," she says. "You must be Brooklyn? Macklin has told us that you'll be staying with us for a while."

And he said no one calls his by his true name. I narrow my eyes at him. He shrugs and leads me to meet his mom.

"Thank you for letting me stay, Mrs. Queen. You have a beautiful home."

"Call me Eliza. A friend in need is always welcome here. And thank you. We try to make it warm and inviting to others." She tugs me forward and embraces me. "Stay as long as you need to, dear." Stepping back, I thank her again. "Macklin. Your father will be back soon, so what are your plans for today?"

"Brooklyn needs to go back home and get some clothes. She packed yesterday but wasn't able to load them into her car. The school isn't safe for her anymore. The boys will try to bring her stuff soon. In the meantime, I loaned her a pair of your pants. I hope that was okay."

"Yes, it's fine dear. Why don't you kids go get her clothes while we wait for Danzel."

"Okay." He nods, turning. "Come on."

I follow him down the stairs and into his bedroom.

"I'm going to shower and change, and then we can go. Do you need to call or text them to let them know we're coming?"

"Yeah, I'll do that and then go shower."

We agree to meet back in his room after we both get ready. I quickly call the house and leave a message with the housekeeper.

McQueen decides to take an SUV since his dad has the Mercedes. I tell him where we're going, but he seems to already know. Does everyone know where I live?

I flash my parking pass to the security officer, and he opens the gate. We ride the private elevator to the fortieth floor. The buzzer indicates our arrival. No one greets us. I didn't expect that they would, but I hear voices coming from the kitchen. McQueen trailing behind me, I walk into the room.

My mom is the first out of her chair and hugs me. "Oh honey, we've been so worried about you. John called us last night and told us a little bit about what happened. Thank the stars you got out in time." She gives me another hug.

Dad comes around and wraps his arms around his wife and me. "At least you're safe now."

I pull back. "I'm not staying here, though. I can't put you guys in harm's way. It's better if you don't know where I am. But I'll text or call you every few days, so you don't worry."

"I'll keep her safe," McQueen says.

"And you are?" Dad asks.

"McQueen. I'm one of her protectors and will be the main one until my brothers leave the school."

"Brothers?" Mom asks.

"Manny, Bronx, and Staten," I say.

"I swear on my dragon's life I will keep your daughter safe." McQueen places a hand over his heart.

Mom nods. She knows what my boys mean to me. While she doesn't know McQueen yet, I hope she trusts me enough to realize that I wouldn't be with them if I didn't think they would honor their words.

"You better mean that," Dad says.

"We got your message, and I left some luggage in your closet.

"Thanks, Mom."

I hug my parents again, heading toward my room. It seems that it was only yesterday I was packing for school. And now I'm bundling my stuff to flee into the arms of the beasts I was training to kill.

Chapter Eight

After my folks tell me again to be safe, and my Dad threatens McQueen again that if he doesn't keep his promise, he'll be in a world of hurt, I find myself heading back over the Whitestone Bridge.

McQueen takes the two suitcases, bringing them to my room. I follow with the lighter, smaller one. Most of my loungewear and everyday clothes are at school. Opting for more practical attire, I grabbed what I could, but left all the gowns, sundresses, and heels at home. I do hope that the boys at least manage to get my garment bag that holds my leather duster jacket and corset: my fighting gear.

By the time we head back upstairs, there is a man sitting at the kitchen table. He has sandy brown hair, broad shoulders, and wears jeans and a polo shirt.

His head tilts back, turning in our direction. Jade eyes greet me—the same ones as McQueen's. "Son," he says.

"Dad." He nods. "This is Brooklyn Bryer. She's the one I've told you about."

McQueen's dad sets his coffee mug down and rises from his chair. He towers over us. Pulling a play out of Staten's book, only his eyes lower.

"So you're the latest Kill Shot turned protector. You found the courage to take on the Slayers' Council?"

"I am." He won't intimidate me. Holding my ground and his eyes, I focus on the man in front of me.

"And who happens to be the most coveted dragon in our species?" He takes a step forward, causing me to lean my head back. I still don't break.

"I am."

"And who is the unofficial Pride Leader?"

My mental connection to them all snaps open for split second. Then I block them out using the technique Staten taught me, slamming the door closed, but not before I get a peek of this man's inner thoughts. "I am." I pick out his voice quickly only because he's talking to me out loud and I can decipher which is his in my mind.

Hum, that's interesting. Hard exterior, but a warm and caring man. I suppose that makes sense.

He nods and waves me to the table. "Welcome to the Pride, Brooklyn. My name is Danzel." He sits and motions for us to do the same. "So, tell me everything from the beginning."

I look at him and then to McQueen, who nods. I regale them with my story of how I first came to York Academy, how I met each of the brothers, and how they came to be my teachers. Then why Staten had brought me into the dream realm to meet the other dragons. I learned that the boys were sabotaging the missions with me by piecing together the odd facts. And finally, I turned into a dragon.

"And what happened at the Council meeting?" he asks.

"I attended with my parents and John. Mr. Astor tried and failed to get us removed from the hearing, saying that my folks would be biased. I told him and the rest of the council the demands. I didn't tell them who any of the dragons are except that I am one. Mrs. Mercer agreed, and then the majority acquiesced."

"After, we took Brooklyn back to her room," McQueen says. "Her parents wanted her to go home, but she needed to pack and tell a few people that she was leaving."

"That's when I got a message from Manny saying that a group somehow found out that I was at the Slayers' meeting and what the Council agreed to. They weren't happy about it, so I fled. I didn't want to bring that to my parents' doorsteps, so McQueen said I could come here. It'd be the safest place for me until we could figure out what our next step is."

"I'm sure that Allister is the one who let it leak," Danzel says. "He's been wanting to reorganize the Council to be more like ours. One leader. He does have a group of supporters who would back him, but your parents have a lot of influence, too. It doesn't surprise me that Allister would try to get students to turn on you. He'll work the Council and them to see you as their enemy."

"Dad, do you think he's going to try and back out of the deal, even though the majority of the Council has agreed to grant the land?"

"He's going to try." Danzel turns in my direction. "How many people were at the meeting?"

"Maybe a little more than a dozen."

"Okay, so half of the Council members. He'll probably try talking to the rest individually and call another vote if it's needed. And not invite our supporters, your parents in particular."

"So what do we do in the meantime?" I ask.

"Mack's brothers are still at the school, and they'll be our eyes and ears. You need to continue practicing shifting and using your magic. I'll call for a Council meeting for later this week. I'll arrange that today. In the meantime, please make yourself at home."

"Thank you."

"Come on, Brooklyn. No time like the present, let's see what you got."

McQueen leads me into the basement. It's three gigantic rooms that seem to be larger than the house. The ceiling has to be higher than fifteen feet tall. There are no windows, save for a few interior doors that look to be closets. The entire rooms are cement and painted white. Nothing hangs on the walls.

He opens one of the doors and holds out blue mats. I take a couple as he grabs two in each arm. We set them on the bare floor. "We'll spar in here. Through that door," he points to his right, "are the treadmills, free weights, and some other exercise equipment. And through that door is a staircase that leads out into the backyard. Don't worry about the noise. This room is soundproof and is double-cemented. Staten said that your dragon is quite large, and I don't know if you'll fit down here in that form. If not, we'll ward the backyard and do more training out there. Otherwise, I'll take you to a remote place." I nod. "Good. Okay, let me see what you've got under that scrawny frame of yours."

It's a good thing I'm in yoga pants and a T-shirt. I tie the extra material into a knot, gather my long black hair into a scrunchie, and attack.

I don't forewarn him. My arms wrap around his solid waist, ramming my shoulder into his hard stomach. He doesn't move an inch. I try sweeping his legs, but he's already anticipated that move. My right fist flies toward his face. He dodges it. My left fist barrels into his side and gets nothing but air.

Continuing with the tactics that Manny and Bronx have taught me, I keep my body moving. McQueen never takes the offensive. In fact, he's barely doing anything on the defensive. My hits, kicks, or punches don't seem to do anything to him.

Here I thought I was doing an okay job in Skills. Clearly, I need help.

Chapter Nine

A grin sweeps across his face. "I see Bronx and Manny have gone soft in your training." He hasn't broken a sweat.

"I'm beginning to think that they both were going easy on me." My forehead and neck have sweat running down. When I see those two next, I'm going to ask them. I guess I understand why they didn't really teach us how to kill the dragons or fight each other. But I needed to know how to do this, and they shouldn't have gone light on my training. "I don't think I even managed to land a punch on you." I'm panting hard.

McQueen shakes his head. "You did, but not enough to do any damage. The technique is there, so we'll need to work on building strength and stamina. Your hits need to pack a punch. I also don't think you're using your magic when you fight." I shake my head. "Which since you've just graduated to be a Level Two, makes sense. You'd be learning to use that more when you move into Level Three."

"Yeah." I inhale. "We were just starting to use magic. I mean, I know it's there, waiting for me to call it. But most of the time when I'm on the offensive, it's uncontrolled and people get hurt. Maybe I'm afraid to use it."

"You shouldn't be. Your magic is a part of you. It's an extension of you and your dragon. Staten might have to continue with that training aspect." McQueen walks toward the closed door. I think he said it was the equipment room. He motions me to follow. "Now that I've seen what you can do, I think it's best that we get into a routine for you. Try to stick to it as best we can. I hope you're an early riser." I nod. "Good, because starting tomorrow, we'll be running between five and ten miles a day, then doing weight training. Every other day, we'll toggle between upper and lower body. Sunday, we'll rest."

I gulp. Staten was the military man, but I think McQueen is putting him to shame. I know I need to do this, so I keep my mouth shut.

"My mom is a health nut, and we don't have any junk food in the house. She lets me indulge in sugar cereals, but I don't eat it all the time. You'll be eating a lot better than what you've probably been used to, especially from the café."

Eating better foods isn't going to be an issue for me.

Now, I feel guilty for eating Peanut Butter Captain Crunch this morning.

"You ready to run?" he asks.

"Yep, let's do this." I step onto the treadmill, and he uses the one next to mine.

We start at a fast walk and gradually increase speed to a jog. Ten minutes into the warm up, the pace is faster. My shorter legs stretch to keep up with his strides. It's not a competition per se, but he knows that my fighting skills were lacking. I can't let him know that my endurance is terrible, too.

It's in these moments I'm grateful that I am a runner. I finally get into a good rhythm, so I can now hold a conversation.

"After this, are we going to practice magic?" I ask.

"Sure, if you'd like. I'm not anywhere near what Staten can do, but Manny, Bronx, and I can hold our own. We can also call the boys to see what's going on and if they plan to stop over today with your stuff."

I nod. "Why don't you communicate with them through your mind?"

He shrugs. "Just never got into it. I talk with them when I have to. You know, emergencies like when I got shot in the park. I didn't have the strength to find my phone and dial one of them. Besides, I don't need to know what they are thinking all the time. I like keeping things private."

"How come you didn't enroll into York?" I ask.

"Staten is always wanting to learn, and what better way than to be at a school. He loves books. The nerd he is."

"I know. I've seen them in his room."

"And Manny and Bronx. They're tight being both nineteen years old; they have that in common. I'm not like my older brother, and the other two usually didn't hang out with me. Sure, I'd probably be in the same Level as them, but it's just different. Plus, I hated normal school. There was no way I was going to attend classes teaching how to slaughter my kin."

Don't I know it. It only took me killing one dragon to know that I couldn't keep doing that in my future. Then seeing others be taken down. Nope, no way. I'm kinda surprised that Manny is able to do it; he has such a big heart.

"Although seeing the weapons facility would have been cool."

"When does that happen?" I ask.

"Usually late in the third year. But since a lot of kids died from the attack the other night, they should look into consolidating classes."

"Speaking of which, why did the dragons come out and attack the school? I mean, I get that they're mad and want to see change, but antagonizing or bullying humans isn't what's going to get us land, so we can live peacefully. It's the exact opposite."

"My dad is the High Councilman, direct ear to the Pride Leader, and since Regan died, we've been lacking a true and strong leader. There are some older dragons that like killing, and we don't have any checks and balances in place. We can't have a civil war if we're going to fight against the slayers. Many of the younger shifters really do want peace, but they won't rise against the elders of the Pride."

We have to get on the same page, have a united front, and I hope we can put the internal battles to rest and focus on the external one that I know is looming in the distance.

Chapter Ten

We end our run and move on to free weights. McQueen selects dumbbells, tells me how many reps, and does his own routine while I work out. About an hour later, we're both dripping in sweat and heading toward the showers. He'll call Staten to see what's going on at the school.

When I'm clean and in fresh clothes, I wander into McQueen's room to wait. Now that it's daylight and I'm not half asleep, I take in the surroundings. He hasn't fixed his bed. The brown comforter is rumpled as if he tosses in his sleep. I notice the room isn't as messy as it was yesterday. Drawers are closed. The desk has been cleared off.

McQueen enters his room with only a towel wrapped around his waist. His body glistens with water as he pats his hair. "Like what you see?" He freezes for a second and then composes himself. "I can tell by your eyes that you do."

I swallow. There's no reason to deny what he said. His half naked body is the stuff legends are made from. Stomach muscles ripple as he stalks closer to me, his legs long and powerful.

Shrugging, I say, "I've seen better." Out of his brothers, he is the most ripped.

A sly grin forms on his face. "Sure you have." He grabs clean clothes from his dresser drawers and saunters back into the bathroom, leaving the door wide open. "Do you want to call Staten and see what's going on? And see if they're coming over today. I would suggest not grabbing your luggage just yet since it's the middle of the day. Maybe doing that at night is better."

"Yeah, sure. I can do that." I pull out my phone and find Staten's number. He picks it up on the second ring. "Hi. I'm putting you on speaker, so McQueen can hear you, too."

"Okay," he says.

"Anything we need to know about?" McQueen asks as he steps out from the bathroom, now fully clothed.

"No, not really. Allister is having a hernia about the Council meeting. He's been locked in his office since yesterday. We went after a couple of the students who were part of the mob last night, but no one seems to know how it got started. Sounds weird to me, sort of like magic was used on them. The school is reorganizing the Levels since there aren't many students left."

"Makes sense."

"Yeah."

"Staten?" I ask. "How's Noelle doing?"

"I'll have Manny go check on her today. We'll all be hanging low for a while. I think we're being watched. We did manage to get your luggage out of your room."

"Thanks. McQueen thinks that you guys should keep my stuff until things die down and when you get a chance, bring it to his house during the night."

Even though it's only been a day, I miss my boys. And I miss Reist and Sax. They didn't need to die. In fact, no one needed to. Not any more if I can stop it.

"Dude, you coming out maybe tomorrow night? If only one of you can sneak off property, no one will notice. Brooklyn still needs magic training. I've restarted her on a workout program because the one Manny and Bronx were doing was piss poor. Her stamina is shit. They've been going easy on her."

"Hey." I slap his arm. "I'm in the room."

"Yeah, I know. Just stating the facts." He sweeps his eyes over my body. "Staten, make sure that you tell them that, too."

"I'll try to get away tomorrow night. Maybe we should alter the schedule and become nocturnal. In the meantime, McQueen, work with her until our sessions resume."

"Got it. Oh, Dad is setting up a meeting for her to meet the dragons. Maybe if she goes to them, they'll keep their noses clean and not be running around the city looking for her."

"Stupid beasts," Staten says. "I get it, though. She's a freak of nature and everyone is curious."

"Hey, jerk," I say. "I'm still in the room."

"I didn't think you left."

"Yeah, well, the next time I see you, you can tell that to my face, and we'll see just what a freak of nature I am."

"I just love her feistiness." McQueen waggles his brows. "You can show me some of that feistiness anytime, Babe. Anytime."

This time I punch his arm. I think my hand is more injured than he is.

"Anything else?" Staten asks.

"No."

"Okay, keep her safe, McQueen."

"I always will."

Chapter Eleven

"What are we going to do now that we know Staten won't be here until tomorrow night?" I ask.

"I can think of one thing."

"Get your mind out of the gutter." I pocket my cell phone into my waistband.

"You love it in there."

I tilt my head. "Maybe. But we need to be productive."

"It's getting more exercise in." He stands, holding out his hand. "Come on, let me show you the rest of the house since we didn't get a chance to last night."

McQueen guides me through the large house. He shows me the library, saying I can read any book in there I find interesting. And there are a ton. Between the history of dragons, the Council, and genealogy, I could be reading for years. Then we make our way to the game/movie room, back to the kitchen, and through the formal dining room that seats at least thirty people. He tells me that's where the

Council meets. And finally, we reach the backyard.

We stand on the deck overlooking the bay. It's quiet out here for the middle of a Wednesday afternoon. Traffic is still heard on the Whitestone Bridge. The sun shines on my face as I tilt it back. I breathe in and relax.

I honestly don't think I've been relaxed since before my Level Two graduation night. It seems that one thing after another keeps rolling in, and we need to address it. I exhale.

McQueen stands behind me, massaging my shoulders. I groan. I don't need to turn around to know he's smiling. Thankfully, he doesn't say anything. I know what he's thinking, anyway. His deft fingers press into my shoulder blades. My head hangs forward as his palms rub my neck.

I think at some point I begin to purr. The sound is met by rumbling behind me. McQueen grabs my shoulders, backing me into his chest. He nips my earlobe and then nuzzles me. I lean my head against him. His arms wrap around my waist. Placing my hands over his, I lay them flat against my stomach.

We're content holding each other. At least our dragons are. He lays his chin on top of my head. I briefly wonder why my dragon was instantly attracted to his when it took a while for her to trust Staten, Bronx, and Manny. The moment I saw McQueen naked in the park, I knew there was something special between us. And then when I met him in the woods, she knew she wanted to be with him.

Maybe it's his protective nature. Maybe it's his confidence. Maybe it's more than that.

And thinking of our dragons, we should practice shifting, flying, and offensive and defensive maneuvers. But I don't want to move away from him. I'm secure in his warm embrace. Protected.

We stay in each other's arms for a while longer, listening to the water lap the shore. Listening to our heartbeats. I inhale his lemongrass fragrance.

I sigh, stepping away from his body. "Let's go into the basement and train in dragon forms. I haven't practiced since we were at the cabin. I need to shift faster and be used to that body."

He nods. "As you wish, Babe."

We walk downstairs, put the mats away, and gather in the large room. I don't know if my dragon form will fit down here, but we should at least try. McQueen is already stripping his clothes off. I guess he doesn't really have a problem with nudity. Growing up a shifter might have made him more comfortable in his own skin.

I, on the other hand, can barely manage to change in front of Noelle. As casually as I can muster, I turn around and peel off my pants and shirt, leaving my undergarments on.

Then I call forth my magic. The greenish flames dance

on my fingertips, tracking along my arm and then over my body as they descend like a blanket. I turn my head toward McQueen, who is already in his dragon form, waiting for me. His tongue rolls out of his mouth as his eyes scan my almost-naked body.

Maybe I should do this by myself. He's making me self-conscious; I know that when I need to change back, I'll be buck-naked. Shaking that thought from my mind, I let the magic seep into me, allowing the change to come. My head drops to my chest. I fall onto all fours. My skin tickles as it morphs into multi-colored green scales. A tail sprouts and a nose elongates. Fingers change into claws. And then a pair of massive leathery wings sprout from my back.

McQueen moves to the corner of the room, giving me ample space to make the shift. Once I'm in my dragon body, I do take up most of the room. I crouch my head, and my tail is curled around my hind legs. I won't be able to do any fighting in this room. Not with the both of us in here.

"Took you long enough, Babe."

I give him a salty look that says, "Shut up." This is why I told him I needed to practice. The boys can change in a matter of seconds, while it takes me almost a minute. It needs to be instant, or at least close to it.

"It'll come faster the more you do it, and the discomfort will also go away," he says.

"I can handle that. I barely feel it now."

"I'll have to take you outside if you want to fight." His large jade eyes roam around the room. He can almost touch his head to the ceiling. Making his way toward me, he slinks along the ground, a submissive posture. My dragon kinda likes that.

"Maybe we'll just practice shifting until I'm as fast as you guys."

"Not a bad idea. It does come in handy at times. I'll stay in this form so your dragon gets used to me."

"Oh, she's already used to seeing you."

"Is she now?"

I shake my head at him, purring sounds from my chest, and I know he hears it. Stupid inner dragon.

Letting my magic course through my body once again, it wraps around me and finally changes me back into a human body. The slight cracking of bones gets easier and easier. My skin doesn't itch like it used to; I've shifted a handful of times now.

When I'm back having two legs and arms, I don't give my brain too long to dwell on the fact that I'm naked, and McQueen's eyes are intense with desire.

My magic doesn't extinguish; I need it right away to change back into the dragon. This time, my thoughts are focused on the change itself. What my body does, what needs to happen. I don't look at McQueen as my green scales reappear.

Chapter Twelve

After practicing changing between dragon and human form to the point where it becomes second nature, I finally shift under five seconds. Almost as fast as McQueen.

I missed lunch, but my body keeps calling for a nap from shifting. "How about a break?" I ask.

McQueen is pulling on his pants. "Sure. You've got to be exhausted."

"I want to learn this, and since there isn't anything else to do …"

"How about we grab a snack, and then if you're feeling up for it later tonight, we can use the darkness, and I can show you some fighting moves."

I nod. Using all of my magic reserves takes a toll, and I need to be in top shape mentally and physically if I'm going to fight and continue with magic lessons with Staten. He and I will need to sort a schedule out, especially if he can't come over here regularly.

Of course, it's never far from my mind the reason why the constant pushing of my physical and magical abilities. A battle looms on the horizon. Or something is coming, and I must be ready.

The much-needed break has done wonders for my body, mind, and soul. I ended up falling asleep for a couple of hours after the late lunch. It's not until I hear a quiet knock on my door that I wake. "Yes?" I say.

"You up?" McQueen says.

I shake the remnants of my sleep away and stretch. "Come in."

The door opens and McQueen grins. "Glad you got some rest. It's just about dusk, and if you're up for it, we can continue our training."

I stifle a yawn and nod. I'm still wearing my clothes from earlier, and they'll do just fine for the evening. I lie there a couple more seconds and then swing my legs off the bed. "All right, let's go."

We walk out of the back door and onto the lawn. The sky is dark navy with the last remaining streaks of reds, oranges, and purples from the sun. The sliver of moon is just peeking above the horizon.

"My father warded the backyard, so we're free to do

what we need to," McQueen says. "He might pop in and give you some pointers and see how training is coming along."

I nod and start stripping out of my clothes before a tail sprouts or the massive wings can appear, destroying my attire. Each time, it's getting easier to be naked in front of my boys. The magic comes forth effortlessly. A snout protrudes before I even get my shoes off. In no time, my dragon body forms and sits on the grass. I'm a split second slower than McQueen. I smile, flashing my long teeth at him.

"Hey, Babe, that's your fastest shift yet. I knew you could do it. With more practice, you'll be changing faster than us."

"You think so?"

He nods. *"Well, maybe not Staten. But it's not a contest."*

"What's the first step?" I slowly advance on his two-toned dragon. He doesn't lower his head in a submissive posture. A growl escapes my lips. My dragon doesn't like that he's not being submissive. Then, he holds it higher. My growls turn into purring. I wish she would stop that. McQueen's nostrils flare as he inhales my scent.

I think back to gym class when Madi handed me my ass, and Bronx should have stopped the fight sooner. *"Go easy on me."* Putting those instructions out there settles me. Almost. *"Just out of curiosity, why am I learning to fight in dragon form? Do we normally fight others of our kind?"*

"Not too often, but it does happen, and as leader you need to be prepared for everything. Bronx told me a bit about what happened at school. So we'll talk through what you'll do first, then I'll show you, and then you can follow along with me." That sounds like a great approach. My dragon thinks so, too. *"Let's have you learn to use your body weight. You're a lot larger than normal male dragons."* His eyes scan my body. *"You should be able to use brute force to get others into submission. Knocking your opponents down and incapacitating them is your first priority. Watching out for their teeth and claws while trying to gain the upper hand is the trick. So I'm going to come at you and try to knock you down. I'll be gentle."*

McQueen takes a few steps toward me. He hunkers down as I watch him in slow motion. *"See how my body is low to the ground? And how my shoulder is leading? You'll want to direct the force into a small, compact punch. Think of it as using a fist to hit someone in their face versus a palm. Both are effective, but the fisted hand hurts more."* He angles his body upward and then gently hits me in my chest, in between the juncture of my leg and shoulder. *"Okay, now you try."*

I lumber toward him, sizing him up. He's right in that I'm taller and broader than he is. But he's used to his dragon form. I'm not. My wings fan out.

"Pull your wings in," McQueen says. *"They'll create drag."*

I do as I'm told, barreling into him. He doesn't budge. Using my head, I ram it into his chest and push. His feet remain planted in the same position. I back up to the outer edge of the lawn, running at him again. It only takes six strides to reach him. Tucking my head low to the ground, I jam my shoulder into his neck.

McQueen's front legs step back. Before I can push him over, he's balanced again.

Boroughs.

While he's smaller than me, his body is solid muscle. I'm not going to toss him using my weight alone, even though he thinks I can. Maybe on a lesser dragon, or one who's inexperienced, or perhaps one I catch by surprise. But not McQueen. He's ready for me.

"While you can use your head like a battering ram, you can hurt yourself if it's not done properly," McQueen says. *"Your neck is a weak point. You could twist it, cut your own air supply off, and in extreme cases, have spinal injuries. Head butting is more often used to stun the other dragon. Let me show you how to use your legs. Remember that you have four of them and a tail at your disposal."* He launches himself up onto his hind legs, paws the air, and slams back into the ground. His actions remind me of how a polar bear stomps on ice. Then his tail sweeps to the side and back again. *"You try."*

Again, I mimic what he did, so I'm used to the movements.

"Good. Now use it on me."

We continue like that well into the night. By the time he

calls it quits, he's demonstrated the areas on a dragon that are the weakest: neck, eyes, and belly. He shows me how to use teeth and claws to scratch, bite, and maim the opponent into submission. McQueen is an excellent instructor. He's patient and not his cocky self. It's probably how he was taught. Or perhaps Bronx told him what happened to me in more detail than what McQueen led me to believe.

Chapter Thirteen

If using magic normally wipes me out, being in my real dragon body is worse. I've used muscles that I didn't know existed. Carrying that extra mass causes my legs, arms, back, and yes, even my neck, to be sore.

After I transform back into my human body, I sway from exhaustion.

"Come on, Babe, let's get you into bed."

"My bed, not yours."

His light chuckle lulls me to sleep. "Of course, that's where I am planning to take you." I swat his arm. "No, really."

My legs give out and warm arms lift under my knees and back. I lay my head onto his shoulder. He gently lays me into a bed, flicking off the light. His footsteps don't wake me.

It doesn't take long for normal dreams to fill my mind with the faces of my school friends: Noelle, Chris, and

Brian. We're all hanging out again in the Lounge, laughing and telling jokes. Even Reist and Sax are there. They are dead now, so I know this isn't real. But to see their faces again, smiling and having fun, soothes me. And then I'm sad because I know when I wake, the reality of them dying will crash into my heart.

Then it's a new dream, memories really, of me and my boys. We're all in a room, watching TV or a movie. I'm nestled between Manny and Bronx. Staten's in a chair, and McQueen lies sprawled on the floor. Manny runs a finger inside my palm. My feet are being rubbed by Bronx. We're happy.

And then the scene changes again into the mountain view I've come to cherish. I know who will be waiting for me. And my instincts are correct.

Staten.

"Hello," he says. *"Glad you could make it."*

"I don't think I have a choice."

"You always have a choice."

"You mean, I don't have to be here?" His wings droop a bit. *"Not that I don't want to be here."* I'm peddling backward. *"It's just that this is new for me, and I didn't know I had the choice."*

"You can block me out and just sleep or have normal dreams. I'm glad you're here, though."

We're both standing on the ledge, overlooking the

landscape. The moon is out, which makes this dream different. I've never been here at night. It's magical with the brighter and larger moon hanging high in the sky. The millions of stars twinkle against the dark blue heavens.

"Me, too," I say.

"What's been going on? Has McQueen been treating you okay?"

"He's been the perfect gentleman."

It's peaceful here. Only the cicadas' voices fill the evening with their songs. All the other animals must be nestled in for the night.

"There's a first for everything." He chuckles.

"We've been training, practicing shifting, and earlier this evening, he taught me to fight in my dragon form."

"Ah, all good stuff to know."

I nod. *"Are you still coming over tomorrow night?"*

"Yes, if that's okay with you."

"Of course it is. I miss you guys. For the past few weeks, we've hung out every day and now all of a sudden, I don't get my daily boys' fix. I think I'm going through withdrawal. Tell me news from school. How's Noelle? Did you guys take instructor positions? What classes are you teaching? Do you have Noelle as a student?"

"Are you going to keep asking me questions, or are you going to let me answer them?" He grins as he lies down. His snout nudges me to do the same. *"We decided that it was best if we*

be instructors. *The Council doesn't know about us. They only know you are a dragon. And if we're here, maybe one of us will get a position on their Council. Perhaps we can infiltrate that way, too. It makes the most sense if it were me. I haven't been seen with you a lot of the time, unless it's for a class, like my brothers."*

My body curls up against Staten's. "You're the best choice because of your magic. Granted, Manny and Bronx would also be excellent choices, too. But you've got the analytical brain." I gaze into the evening sky, across the fields and over the snow-capped mountains.

"That may be," Staten says. *"I'm teaching the Level One and Two magic classes. John has been let go from his position because he sided with your parents."*

My stomach flips. Oh, boroughs. The school sacked him for knowing and associating with me? That's not right. Makes me glad I'm not part of that any more, even though I miss my friends and boys. *"Manny is teaching social media, which I still get a kick out of, and Bronx is continuing with Skills."*

"When do you think you'll know if you're invited to be on the Council?"

"Probably soon because a couple members died during the fight, and they want to replace them. Rumor is that Allister is holding secret meetings, so he can get sympathizers to his side. If we play our cards right, I could use that. I might be young, but

I'm a three year in a row Kill Shot, book smart, and one of their finest magical users they've had in years."

We curl up together and lie on the ledge, watching the moon rising higher into the sky. We stay there until the early morning sun's rays replace the darkness. It doesn't feel like a lot of time has passed. Maybe time has no meaning here in this dream world of Staten's.

For now, I'm content being with him like this. Like we normally are.

Chapter Fourteen

By the time the dream sun is high in the sky, I fade away and sleep soundly. But then gory images replace the calm, scenic views.

A field is covered in pools of blood. The trees drip fat red drops, adding to the already saturated ground. Human bodies lie on the blood-soaked earth, limbs akimbo. Skin has been peeled away from deadly claws.

Enormous dragon forms also lay scattered. Their scales glisten like rubies. The sun is out and warms the air, but a stillness blankets the area.

A land of death.

I have no idea where it is, or if it's real or not. But then like a motion picture, the scene rewinds.

Human bodies lift to standing positions. Dragons take flight into the skies. Arrows, bullets, and spears return to their users. Steps retreat to two sides of the field. Large shadows reduce to small specks on the horizon.

No sounds are heard—a quiet before the storm. A battle is brewing that I know will start soon, having just witnessed the end game of destruction.

Slayers are on one side and dragons descend from the other. Silver tipped weapons are out and on the ready to meet their targets.

I'm standing in the middle, watching them rush toward me. Battle cries flick on as if someone turned up the volume. Roars sound from my right, followed by streams of fire.

The land becomes scorched.

Humans run fearlessly to the enemy line. They pass through me like I'm a ghost witnessing the fight that's already taken place, and this is only a memory.

Dragons fly in formation above, and as they near the ground, scatter to make themselves harder targets. They pick off lone bodies lagging behind.

Every warrior on the field is dressed in silver armor. My guess is it's all made from titanium. Their only protection. But I know that it doesn't stop their deaths. The dragons find a way to slay them all.

Bullets soar as a volley of arrows launch into the skies, some hitting the delicate, leather-like wings.

Human lines form and advance on the creatures that land, now battling on the ground. Being too smart to get caught by the people's nets and lines, aerial dragons blow fire between the groups, not allowing for the people to continue their progression.

As the wall of fire diverts the people, the dragons continue to snatch them unawares, killing them instantly. The humans gather into tight groups, shields up to protect them from burning.

Screams penetrate my ears and nestle into my soul. I know what a death shout sounds like. This isn't my first battle, nor will it be my last.

The smell of flesh charring fills my nose as I watch a body run past me, still burning. I wish he would drop and extinguish the flames, but it won't do any good.

Flame throwers line up, ready to launch their attack. People ready their special crossbows. I've never seen anything like it before. A single bow has seven arrows notched and ready. Dozens of them take aim for targets across the field. Someone yells "fire," and the arrows are let loose.

A second line rushes and fires while the first line reloads their bows. It's a massive destruction to the dragon forces. The sharp points slam into their bodies, chests, open maws, and wings. They are dropping from the skies. The grounded ones are dying from easy kill shots.

The dragon magic swirls in the air and mixes with the humans. Some is being absorbed back into the ground while other tendrils float in the air, finding new forms to mesh with.

Five green dragons stand on a ledge overlooking the battle. I didn't notice them before. The front one is tall while the other four smaller ones flank its sides.

It's me and my protectors.

We watch as our forces are decimated just as badly as our opponents. Black smoke rises from burning trees, grass, and human bodies.

A screech escapes my lips. Only a few remaining dragons turn their heads to my cry. My wings expand, and I leap off the cliff gliding down to the open field. My boys follow.

I survey the carnage.

The remnants of magic flows into me.

My brown eyes scan the waste of life. It didn't need to come to this. We had a truce. They broke it.

I'm focused on my fallen brethren and don't hear humans approaching. Not until it's too late. One of my boys calls out a warning but not in time. Staten and Manny take to the sky, leaving Bronx and McQueen guarding me.

Those silver tipped arrows are out and pointed at us. All of my protectors launch fireballs at the approaching humans. They lift their shields, hiding from the flames.

We take defensive positions. I call out a warning to them. The people don't stop. They fire their weapons.

McQueen launches himself in front of me, taking

multiple arrows to his chest and belly as he rears up. Bronx's wings are shredded, but he's still moving. His tail sweeps the line of people, battering them down, while Staten and Manny continue their assault from the sky and behind the human line.

The people reload their arrows as a barrage of bullets come raining down on us. Manny falls from the sky.

The arrows are ready and firing again, taking Bronx from me, too.

Staten lands in front of me.

Somehow, I've always known it would come down to him and me. Our relationship is the most unconventional, but really there is nothing normal about any of this. But he's here now, doing his job. Fighting alongside me. The Pride Leader.

More than a dozen humans remain, still firing at us with everything they have.

I don't take the quick second to mourn my boys. Rage fills my heart as the humans take away my loves. I'll never see them again. Never feel their hands on my flesh. Never know their dragon magic.

I go on the offensive and ram through their lines. My tail sweeps back and forth. My claws are out, digging into a few soft bodies.

Staten is doing the same. We've killed all but a few of them. But he's hurt. His stride is short and he's limping.

I'm not much better. My wings have gaping holes in them, casting dots on the ground. We're making our last stand here. Now.

The trees move. No, not the trees, bodies move behind the tree line. More humans run out, firing arrow after arrow from those deadly crossbows.

Staten goes down. His eyes close for the final time.

A shrill cry bursts from my throat. And with my last breath of air, I summon all of my magic, all of my essence and being. I direct it at the humans. Humans who betrayed me and my kind.

They don't deserve to live.

As I feel my heart beat slowing, I expel my bright green magic. It floods the field, ricocheting around like a pinball machine. The force of it packs a punch as it sweeps through the slayers, knocking them onto the ground and absorbing their magic—leaving them with nothing. Their hearts no longer beat.

Just like my own.

Chapter Fifteen

A scream wrenches from me and I jerk awake.

The door swings open, and McQueen stands in the doorway, fists clenched and scanning the room for an intruder. When his jade eyes land on me, they examine my body. Seeing that no one is with me and I appear to be unhurt, he strides forward. "Are you okay?" he asks. "I heard your scream."

I nod. I can't speak. The memories are still too fresh in my mind. I died. My boys died, protecting me. The whole Pride died. The slayers died on the bloody battlefield.

My body shivers. Tears swell in my eyes.

McQueen walks farther into my room and sits on the bed. "It'll be all right." He pats my foot. I've never seen him like this before, unsure of himself. "Do you want to talk about it?" He's sweet, keeping his voice low.

I shake my head as my arms wrap around my legs, bringing them closer into my chest. I lay my head on my knees.

He motions for me to move over, crawling under the covers to sit next to me. His body is warm, strong, and now I feel safe. Comforted.

I lay my head on his shoulder as he tucks me into his side. We stay like that for a while as I get my breathing under control. Eventually, it evens out and I can form coherent thoughts. "I had a dream," I whisper, cringing at my next words. "There was a battle. We all died." I suck in a breath. "As in you boys, me, and the slayers. Everyone. I don't know if it was real or something that will happen. But it felt real. I felt those souls die. I felt my Pride's voices go quiet."

"Do you know where it happened?"

I've never seen the place before. Nothing looked familiar. There weren't any distinguishing landmarks. "No," I say.

"It's just a dream." He squeezes my shoulder and swings his legs off the bed.

"McQueen?"

His eyes find mine. "Yeah?"

"Will you stay with me?"

A grin spreads across his face. He swallows. "I thought you'd never ask." His eyes twinkle.

"To sleep."

"Whatever you want, Babe."

I'm still rattled about the fight and the deaths. But eventually sleep finds me in the warmth of McQueen's arms. I don't know if he sleeps at all. His breathing never changes. I think he is still awake when I drift into a restless slumber. He's staring at me when I wake, too.

His fingers brush my hair from my face. "Better?" he asks.

The morning sun streams in through the blinds. It's going to be a great day. I won't let the lingering bad feelings I have dampen my thoughts. Tonight, Staten is coming over to continue magic training. Maybe he'll bring his brothers, and they can hang out.

"Yeah, I think so," I say. "Thank you for staying with me last night." I glance at the window, not wanting to face him.

"It's not a problem. I love being with you." He shrugs. "Sure, we've only been hanging out for a couple of days, but we have a connection that neither of us can deny. When my brothers found you, I knew that I'd be the last to link with you. I'm just glad that your dragon *really* likes mine." He smiles. Perhaps his brothers told him what they had to go through to get my dragon to like theirs. "She's a smart one, I'll give you that. And what's not to like about me?" He sweeps his hand down his body. "I mean, hello."

"Conceited much?"

"Only a little bit." He smirks. "I know it's probably early, but I want to get this out there. I know you're dating

Manny and Bronx. Not sure what's going on with Staten, but I know that you two have something special, or should I say, weird between you. They told you that they don't mind sharing you, and I'm just tossing in my own name in there, too. I think since your dragon has the hots for me, that maybe our human forms should ... you know." He nods. "Have something, too?"

I blink. He wants to have a relationship with me, too? While I still sort of find it strange dating two guys—and yes, whatever is going on with Staten and me brings it to a whole other level—I feel that I should give McQueen a chance. He's right that our dragons really get along. Perhaps we're supposed to be together. That book that Staten showed me seems to think we should be.

"You might have some reservations about all of this." He turns to face me and leans on his elbow. "Have you ever watched *The Bachelorette*?"

"As in the TV show?"

He nods. "Yeah, where the girl tries to find a husband in the twenty-five contestants. While we are only four, the concept is the same. She goes on dates with everyone, finding that one guy. And in our cases, you don't have to settle on just one. You can have us all."

I like that analogy. He's right. The woman in that show does date multiple guys over the course of the season. She kisses them, sometimes has sex with certain ones. They do dinner outings, movies, sporting events, all while trying to find love.

The best part of what I have is that I've found love in each of them. I don't need to choose between them.

I won't. They all are part of me.

Chapter Sixteen

Today has been low-key; the lingering memories still haunts me. McQueen and I worked out in the morning and then practiced shifting.

It's after dinner when the doorbell rings.

McQueen goes and opens the door. There, standing on the threshold, are all three of my boys. Grins light their faces. They didn't tell me through our bond that Manny and Bronx were coming with Staten.

And now that I see them, here before me, I smile. My heart warms as I fling my arms around each one. "Hi guys," I say. "What a nice surprise. I was only expecting Staten tonight."

"We know," Manny says. "But not much has been going on at the school, and we thought a few hours away won't hurt. Staten told us that he clued you in on the goings on."

"Plus," Bronx says. "We come bearing gifts." He hands me a garment bag. I clutch it to my chest. Yes, my warrior outfit. "Couldn't pass on an opportunity to hang out with you either. Things will get back to normal at York soon, and we don't know when the next time will be we can visit. We might not be able to sneak away. Everyone knows that you're dating me and Manny, and they might be watching us, so they can get to you."

"We drove around the city for over an hour." Staten brushes past me. "We stopped for dinner, circled back to make sure we didn't have a tail on us." He slaps his brother on the back. "You could let us in instead of hanging out there like idiots."

"Sorry, man," McQueen says. "You lived here, too. You don't need an invitation. I'm surprised you even knocked."

"This hasn't been my home for three years."

"That was your choice to make, dude. You're the one who decided to leave and attend York. Not me. I'd offer you guys food but since you already ate dinner, I suppose you and Brooklyn should start training. We'll keep each other company and later, if there's time, we can hang out for a while."

I follow Staten into the basement while the others wander to McQueen's room. I would've liked to spend some time with them, but I know practicing magic is the priority. Later this evening, McQueen suggested that we continue lessons in fighting, especially after I told him a bit more of the dream I had, so that'll be the time I can hang out with all of them.

Staten and I drag out the padding, so we're not sitting on the hard cement. Sitting cross-legged from each other, I get into a comfortable position. I'm not sure what he has planned for tonight. Since he's training me, I wait for him to speak first. When he continues to remain silent, I take the plunge.

"So," I say.

"How," he says at the same time.

"Go ahead." I motion for him to continue.

"No." He shakes his head. "Ladies first."

"I was just going to ask what we'll be doing tonight."

"And I was going to ask you how you've been doing. You look well and rested. Maybe getting away from school has been a good thing."

"Possibly. It's too early to tell, though. I miss Noelle and the Smarties, but then again not being able to see Sax and Reist, it makes me sad. I want to fight more and keep everyone alive. McQueen and I have been training and practicing shifting. We'll continue later this evening, after you guys leave. So that brings me back to my question. What am I learning today?"

"I thought we could try protections and stuns. I think you've done a couple of stuns already. At least that's what Manny and Bronx described it as."

"When was that?"

"On the roof of the girls' dorms. That massive magic ball that shot out over the courtyard. I wasn't there to witness it, but from what the boys described, to me it was a stun."

I nod, thinking back to the other day when the dragons came out and brought the battle to the school. It was the evening when Reist was killed, just when we came back from burying Sax.

Of course, I remember the force of it. Remember how my magic coursed through my body. I was angry for not doing anything, being unable to stop the dragons from killing the slayers. The devastation I felt when the slayers fired back against my kin.

Then the magic exploded out of me on the rooftop. My body glowed bright green. A bubble blasted out from the palms, lighting everything in the area in a faint green glow. It was like a shock wave.

"Yeah, I recall doing it," I say. "I didn't know what it was or why it happened."

"Most of your powers have been emotionally driven. It happens to some but not everyone. When your feelings are extreme, sometimes magic manifests and your control won't be there. We'll also work on breathing techniques. You could injure others and cause harm to yourself if we don't take proper precautions. That will take us into next week as long as you continue, even when I'm not here. McQueen can help."

I slow my breathing, recalling the same instructions from Mr. Lorimer when we became Level Twoers. In. Out. In. Out. Placing my wrists on my knees, I straighten my back and breathe. I concentrate on Staten's breathing, his sandalwood scent, and his hazel eyes staring at me.

"When you're ready, I want you to call your magic and create a bubble around yourself," he says. "Think of it as a flexible shield that bends to your wishes. Have it stretch around your body."

Staten opens his palm and shows me his flame. It hovers and then grows, expanding into the size of a balloon. Eventually, it wraps around his tall frame. The magic extinguishes, but I know it's still there. Invisible.

I mimic his actions. My bright green flame flickers and rises into a tiny sphere. I send more power into it, careful not to pop it. The sides expand, but it won't settle around me. It hovers in front of my face like a shield. No matter what I do, it won't mold into me.

"Keep trying," Staten says. "This is complex stuff. I didn't think you'd get it on the first try. Now, that would be impressive. Most third years aren't doing this."

I nod. At least I created a shield. I'll keep working it. It's like training a new muscle that didn't exist before. Plus, if most Level Threes aren't where I'm at, then I'm already ahead of them. Not that it's a contest or anything. I shouldn't be so hard on myself. But I need to learn and handle this. Lives depend on it. Not only mine, the Pride's and the Slayers.

"So keep practicing that and try to get your shield to flow around you," Staten says. "If you master that before I can come back here, expand it to encompass others. Get McQueen to assist. Since I don't want to get blasted from you." He moves to sit beside me. "Let's work on offensive stuns. I thought it'd be easier for you to learn shields first, and they are considered defensive maneuvers."

He's close, knees barely brushing against mine. I assume that he's doing that on purpose; he knows it's easiest for me to have contact and absorb magic that way. But he once told me not to rely on that because there could be times when I don't have the luxury of someone else to help me.

Without him saying anything, I call my flames into my open palms. He nods and does the same. "Let it simmer. Build it up. And when you're ready, steady your breathing and push it outward."

I do as I'm told, letting my magic hover. Glancing at Staten's hands, I watch his flames dance between his knuckles. It reminds me of those people who can move a coin between fingers. I control my breaths and release.

My magic is quick and fast. Potent. It slams into the far wall, crumbling some of the cinder blocks. Staten turns to face me and I grin. I didn't expect that to happen. I didn't even put that much force into it.

"Oops," I say. "Sorry."

He chuckles. "I'm glad I moved. That was a bit too much magic. You could use that if you really wanted to kill someone, but we're not about that. It's called stunning for a reason. Reign it in, Brooklyn." He nods. "Again."

We continue training for another hour or so. And in that time, I managed not to destroy the walls any further. The force continues to thump, causing them to vibrate. With what we've witnessed previously to the house, it confirms that I really do need to keep practicing, learning, and figuring out my magic.

Chapter Seventeen

We finally call it quits and find the rest of the boys hanging out in McQueen's room. I duck out quickly, informing them that I'm taking a shower and will return.

When I'm finished, I find everyone sitting in the living room. Danzel has joined them. They're chatting away and as I step into the room, all eyes land on me. Silence.

"What's going on?" I ask.

Manny stands and takes my hand, leading me to the sofa. "Maybe you should sit."

"I don't like the sound of that."

"It's not bad," Staten says. "We found out more about the graphic I showed you the other week. You remember?"

I nod. How could I forget? In some old tome, my dragon form is surrounded by four others. My boys. And when Staten showed me it, my magic flared and the picture animated. Their wings flapped as smoke billowed from their snouts. A line connected between them and me.

"Good," Staten continues. "I told Dad about it and what happened."

"We think in order for you to become the Pride Leader, you need to find some very old magic," Danzel says. "Magic that will assist you in being the leader of New York. While other PLs in the world may help, there is a secret society that was created specifically for them. There isn't too much we normal dragons know about the duties and their abilities."

"So, I'm to find another Pride Leader of another clan and ask about the society?" I ask. Everyone in the room nods. "And they're just going to give me that information?"

That seems way too easy. And I'm already Pride Leader, aren't I? That's what Regan told me, right before he died. Some of his magic passed to me. And when I finally acknowledged that I was a dragon to the Slayers Council, my mind opened, and I could hear other dragon voices — besides from my boys.

"I highly doubt they will." Danzel stands. "They might start you on the path, but it'll be up to you to take the journey."

"And I'll be on this quest by myself?" I ask.

"Of course not," McQueen says. "I'll go with you."

"I actually think you four need to go," Danzel says as he turns to look at the boys. "You are, after all, her protectors."

"If we do this," Staten says. "It means that we'll be

leaving the school. Permanently. There is no going back from this." They all nod. I don't think they really want to be there, anyway. I know they'd rather be with me, to watch over and protect me. "Let's get Noelle here and massage her into being our spy while we're out and about," Staten continues.

"That I can do," I say. "When do we leave?"

"As soon as possible. The Council is meeting here in a couple of days. That should allow plenty of time for the boys to get their affairs in order."

Quiet descends upon the room as we all think about our next move. I need to decide how I'm going to approach Noelle. Since she has no magic, she still could remain at the Academy and become an instructor. Eventually, they won't allow her out on missions, even if she graduates to Level Three. Being surrounded by others with magic does allow her to see the dragons, but by herself she won't see us.

"Well, I'll let you guys hang out." Danzel leaves the room.

"It's good to see you again, Brooklyn." Manny comes and sits beside me. "I know it's only been a few days, and I'm sure I say this for Bronx and Staten, too, but we've missed you. We liked seeing you every day, but we're relieved that you're here and safe with McQueen."

"Thanks, Manny. I miss you guys like crazy, too. It's

been good here. McQueen and I have been training, so that keeps my brain from remembering the horrors of why I'm here in the first place. And when I'm alone at night, I do recall the battle. I think it's good that I'll always remember. Someone should remember them. Their sacrifice. Their lives."

"And that is why you'll be a great Pride Leader," Bronx says as he comes to sit on my other side. "The rest of tonight, let's just hang out, be normal, and tomorrow we'll start walking down our new path. In the meantime, you and McQueen should research the other PLs and get some background information."

"What do you guys know about the other leaders?"

"Around the world, there are about seven who lead the different Prides," Staten says. "Their numbers vary but New York is one of the larger ones. Since the beginning, there have only ever been male leaders so you, Brooklyn, will be the first female. We'll want to figure out which one will be the most accommodating toward us." Staten walks to the back of the couch, placing his hands on my shoulders. He squeezes them and takes the recliner. "Dad should be able to help with names and locations on where to find most of them. But some don't want to be found, and others may not help."

"How about we have a bonfire outside?" McQueen says. "We can watch the moon rise, listen to the city's pulse, and if we're lucky, some boats may pass by in the harbor."

I decide to add layers while the boys grab chairs and start the fire. When I walk into my room, the jewelry the boys gave to me for my birthday beckons. I'm not sure what pulls me to them, but I need to brush my fingers along the cool metal. All four of them pulse with something. Magic maybe? As soon as I'm close enough to reach out to them, my own flames appear, mixing with their strange calling. Images flash in my mind, too fast to even figure out that it's showing me. They are blurry enough that I can't make out anything. All I know is that they're important. They're not only special to me because my boys gave them as a present, but more.

I need to ponder on that later. After grabbing a hoodie, I stroll into the backyard. Five chairs are sitting around the campfire, which now is blazing in the cooling night air. One seat between Bronx and McQueen is left for me.

Staten is the only one able to legally drink, but that doesn't seem to stop any of them who have bottles of beer in their hands. McQueen offers me one as I approach. I shake my head, not wanting Manny to be the only one who isn't drinking tonight.

I am curious why Manny doesn't touch the stuff. Bronx had told me that he couldn't hold his liquor and went on some sort of rampage around the city. Now, thinking back on it, Bronx never said if it was in his human or dragon form when he caused so much destruction. I do know that sometimes when emotions run high, the inner beast takes control. It could also be that since Manny is the youngest, he might not have as much control over his dragon. And with drinking, that lowers his inhibitions and reasoning.

"You remember that one time," Bronx says, "when we went four-wheeling in upstate? Gosh, Manny and I must have been what, ten years old? We found that old, dilapidated house in the woods."

"Yeah, you guys didn't go to sleep for over a week," McQueen says.

"Why?" I ask.

"They got scared," Staten says, chuckling. "We dared them to go inside, have a look around. As soon as they went through the door, McQueen and I went around back. Hid until we heard them coming into the kitchen. I had a bit of magic early on and was just practicing moving objects. It wasn't anything to brag about, but I could call up wind. So I used that to move the ripped curtains. I sucked out most of the air in the room, so it was super still and quiet. By the time those two arrived, they were shaking so hard, I thought at least one of them would piss their pants."

McQueen laughs. "Yeah, and just to really make sure one of them did," McQueen says. "I found some old fishing line and tied it to the door knob and cabinets. So when those two actually came into the kitchen, they felt something strange. With Staten removing the air and making the curtains blow, those two were trembling like little girls." I scowled at him. "Sorry, Brooklyn. But then I opened random cabinets."

"I don't know which one screamed first. But they ran into each other and tried to get out of the house as fast as they could," Staten said. "It was like a cartoon. They fumbled around and couldn't figure out how to get out of the room fast enough. It only really was a couple of seconds, but it seemed longer than that. They were about to step through when McQueen slammed the door on them."

"They ran through the entire house. We barely managed to get to the front yard in time to see them running out like they were on fire."

"That was not cool," Manny says. "I still can't go into old houses. You traumatized me. Fools."

I can see McQueen pulling a stunt like that. But it's nice knowing that Staten, too, has a fun side. Hearing them tell stories makes me love them even more. How they grew up together and have each other's backs. I can see in their eyes that they love each other as family, even though Staten and McQueen are the only ones who share blood. The way each relaxes in his chair speaks of their connection; even Staten slouches a bit.

Chapter Eighteen

The sun is almost rising by the time we call it a night. No one seems to want to leave. Because if we do, it means we are acknowledging that today is a new day, and our lives will change forever.

The boys are quitting today. Instead of handing in letters of resignations, they decided to just stop going and slip out. Pack only the things they can't live without and leave. But only after I give them the word that Noelle has agreed to my request.

I need to get Noelle pulled out of school, so I can have a chat with her and convince my best friend that she needs to spy for us. We're starting our new mission in two days.

I hug Manny, Bronx, and Staten, wishing them good luck. McQueen and I see them off. I hope they get a few hours of sleep before their world is turned upside down.

Even though we've been up all night, I'm not tired and suggest to McQueen that we still work out. I can take a nap later, but I need to continue building up muscles so when I'm in my dragon form, her weight and movements aren't so exhausting. And after my nap, I plan to work on using magic, just how Staten showed me last night.

The next morning, Danzel stops by the basement to remind us that the Dragon Council meeting is tonight. And that reminds me that I need to chat with Noelle. I don't want her coming to the house, especially tonight since there will be a bunch of dragons in the house. Maybe she can come over tomorrow morning before we start our journey.

McQueen and I have continued weapon skills and endurance training. He's almost as bad as Bronx in pushing me to the limits, but that's where the similarities end. McQueen, unlike his cocky exterior and brazen behavior, is patient and explains techniques thoroughly, almost to the point that it's overkill. Just like the nights when we're in our dragon bodies, he shows me different maneuvers. He'll tell me in my mind what he is going to do, shows it to me, and then has me try on my own.

That's what we're doing as we end this morning's session: hand to hand combat. The only difference is that McQueen is speaking instructions out loud.

He's demonstrating soft spots on the human body. Target the eyes, throat, chin, and groin. Hits don't have to be hard, but they do have to be direct.

I'm not sure why we're doing this since most of the time, slayers won't be in hand to hand combat against dragons. And since they don't know who the dragons are in human form, it doesn't matter. But I don't voice my opinions. McQueen probably has a reason. Besides, it is a good idea to know some moves just in case. After all, this is the big city, and walking down the street could find you in a not-so-nice situation.

I may be thin and lanky, but that doesn't mean that I'm not fit. During my whole first year, I trained every day. Then the boys came into my life and turned it upside down. Workouts seemed to halt for a while. It's nice being back into a routine.

McQueen holds me from behind. I try to focus on his voice and not the fact that his body is pressed against mine. The heat can be felt through our clothes. "If you find yourself in this position, the easiest way to get out of it is to stomp on the assailant's foot," he says. "All you need is a second to wiggle free, turn, and then slam your palm into the neck." He spins me around so that I'm behind him and then shows me the move. "Now you try."

I stand in front of him again, stomping my foot on his shoes. It's not hard because I don't want to hurt him. His grip around my arms and chest loosen. I twist to face him and then ram the base of my palm into his neck. It doesn't even connect because I pull the punch. I only want to show McQueen I'm doing it correctly.

"Good. Again. These actions need to become second nature."

"Why are we learning this?" I ask. Apparently, I can't hold my tongue about it.

"Because we are going out to find dragons in other Prides. Some aren't going to take lightly about us prying into their leaders' lives. They protect their own. While we will fight some in dragon forms, they might also be in their human bodies. We, of course, will protect you as much as we can, but this is just a precaution. We need to know that you can hold your own until one of us can help you."

"I'm not defenseless. I can—"

"We'd feel better if you just allow us to do this for you. For our peace of our minds."

"Fine. But don't treat me like some damsel in distress. You guys might have more muscles and training, but I can hold my own." I think. "I know when to ask for help or guidance."

"Wouldn't dream of calling you that, ever."

He shows me more ways to escape a hold, and what would happen if there were two assailants. We break and then get on the treadmills, running for miles.

It's early afternoon by the time we've emerged from our showers. McQueen is leaning against the counter making us some lunch. I've already told him that I need to practice magic before the Council meeting, and if we can squeeze it in, more shifter training. Since it's so nice outside, I suggest that we eat on the deck and then use the backyard for magic.

After we eat our sandwiches, I lead him onto the grass and position myself exactly the way I sat with Staten, only McQueen sits beside me. "It's safer this way," I say.

He nods and doesn't say anything more.

Immediately, the flames of my magic are floating on my opened palm. My brain empties and my body relaxes. I don't tell McQueen what I'm doing. Maybe he'll figure it out, or maybe he doesn't care.

His eyes are closed, letting me do what needs to be done. I wonder if he can feel my magic swirling around us?

My hands hum, itching for the magic to be released, to do my bidding. I focus my thoughts only on creating a shield in front of me. The flame flickers and hovers, gradually growing larger. I coax it to become more powerful but not too much. I don't need to be killing the grass, nor the buildings on the other side of the bay. Could my stun reach that far? I don't need to try that. Yet.

All I want to do is to fling my magic shield away from us, using enough force to stun. Not destroy.

"The forcefield around the backyard will hold, right?" I ask.

McQueen's eyes open and land on mine. He nods. "I saw what you did in the basement. Don't worry about it. We'll get the wall fixed. Do your best damage out here." He grins. "In fact, do your worst. I want to see how potent you really are. Maybe we don't have to worry so much about you if your magic is where I think it is."

Maybe he's right. I should try his way and then once I get the feeling of how much power I'm supposed to use, I'll reign it in.

Closing my eyes, I let myself build magic. Flames engulf my mind and body. I can feel McQueen's intense gaze still on me. He knows I can do this. It's that assuredness that I use to continue growing my magic. My face flushes. My body starts to sweat.

Bright green light streams from every pore of my skin. I'm tossed backward. I turn my head and see that McQueen is also on his back. A smile creeps on his face as he looks at me. For a split second, his gaze darts down to my lips. I swallow. Hard.

Whatever magic force is used in the backyard, it absorbs my flames. The outer walls crackle with power. But not before the trees are leveled, the grass smokes, and the potted plants are destroyed.

"I think if you can use that, no one will decide to mess with you." McQueen winks. "That is more powerful than Staten's, well, anything he's let us see." He helps me sit up.

"Dang, Brooklyn. Remind me never to really piss you off."

His warm hand still holds mine as we survey our surroundings. Thinking I could fix the yard, I summon my flames and gently push it outwards, concentrating of healing the grass. Turning it back to lush green. Having the tree upright and standing tall again. Adhering the shattered flower pots. Everything rights itself. Good. I feel bad enough that part of their house was destroyed by me.

McQueen's eyes meet mine again. He swallows this time. Ever since the first night in the woods when he kissed me without my permission, he's never attempted it again. Granted, I did yell at him never to kiss me again unless I tell him it's what I want.

From the heat in his eyes, I can tell he desperately wants to. But he won't ask. He's waiting for me to let him know it's okay. Is it, though? Do I want to kiss him? I think I can handle another relationship with the last brother. There is definitely an attraction I feel toward him.

Chapter Nineteen

McQueen suggests that we get ready for the Council meeting. I use that time to text Noelle.

Me: Hey, there. What's going on? Miss me yet? You want to meet tomorrow morning?

I'm digging in my closet when I hear the ping from my phone.

Noelle: OF COURSE I MISS YOU LIKE CRAZY!!!
Me: Coffee tomorrow?
Noelle: Sure. When and where?
Me: Off campus. There's a bistro about three miles away. Do you know the unmarked path behind the girls' dorm? There is a gate at the end of the property. Use that to leave the school then catch an Uber.
Noelle: Okay. Why so secretive?

Me: I'll tell you more tomorrow.

Now that I've locked in plans with Noelle, I select dark jeans and a blue knit sweater. Laying them on the bed, I walk toward the bathroom and get ready. While the Slayers meeting was informal, I don't know how this meeting will be. Then again, that meeting was an impromptu gathering right after a deadly battle.

The dragons are meeting in a lovely home, and I suspect the entire Council will be here tonight. Especially, since so many of my Pride are curious about me. I met Manny's and Bronx's parents the other week, but there'll be more members I don't know.

I'd rather dress nice than give off the wrong impression. I'm done styling my hair when a knock on the door sounds. I pull it open, and McQueen stands on the threshold. He scans me up and down. My stomach flips seeing him in black pants and a fitted knit shirt. Backing up, I let him into the room.

The room is suddenly smaller with him in it. Or perhaps he's overwhelming my senses. The spark of magic that ping pongs between us is fleeting.

"You ready?" he asks. I nod. It's the only thing I can do. "Good." He holds out his hand. I tentatively step to his side, glancing up to meet his jade eyes. He inhales and squeezes my fingers.

Gently placing his hand at the small of my back, he leads me up the stairs to the formal dining room. He opens the double doors. There seated at the head of a long, mahogany table is his father, Danzel. To his right is Manny's father, Daniel, and to Danzel's left is Bronx's dad, David. They have first names that start with D, and I briefly wonder if they grew up together as children, too.

All eyes glance at the newcomers in the room, and then a hush falls on everyone's lips. There are about a dozen men, not including McQueen, spanning between the ages of what I think is from the low forties to upper sixties.

I feel self-conscious that everyone is staring at me, but then I think that maybe no female has ever attended these meetings. They're curious why McQueen and I are both there. I wring my hands, but then McQueen threads his fingers through mine, stopping my nervous habit. He pulls out a chair for me directly opposite to his father, taking the seat next to me.

"Welcome, Brooklyn," Danzel says as he stands. He turns to face his council. "This is Brooklyn Bryer. And she's the only female dragon alive."

A gasp fills the room. Some try to cover their response with hands, while most others can only stare. A few flares of magic burst through and I know that they can't control it when they're around me.

"How do you know?" someone to my right asks. "I

mean, I can see that she's a female, but how do you know she's a dragon?"

"Can you not feel the pull toward her? I saw a few of your magic flare up when she stepped into the room," Danzel says. "Plus, my sons have been training with her these last couple of weeks. Once she was brought here, I confirmed it with my own eyes." He motions to me. "Brooklyn, would you like to tell your story?"

Oh, my gosh. I should've prepared something ahead of time. Now, my face is burning and whatever comes out of my mouth is probably going to be a garbled mess. My heart rate pulses, and a tiny bead of sweat forms on my forehead.

The boys must be able to feel my sudden spike in emotions. I hear McQueen tell them that everything is okay, and we're at the Council meeting. Their voices float into my mind, caressing it to calm down and relax. Before any other dragon voices can break through the mental barrier, I erect the mental wall once again.

McQueen's warm hand grips my knee from under the table, shaking me to remember that everyone is waiting on me.

I nod to Danzel and stand. "Hello." I suck in a deep breath. "I enrolled into York Academy after I turned seventeen and met Manny Lauren. During graduation into Level Two, I became the Kill Shot." Muffle cries escape from some members. "After that night, Manny introduced me to Bronx and Staten. Then as my magic manifested, John Lorimer told me that I should take personal sessions with Staten since he'd never seen anyone do what I was doing at my age. I started having dreams of myself being a dragon, and I didn't know what it meant, nor that Staten was giving me those dreams. Eventually, I met McQueen here. All four boys helped me change into my dragon form."

"So my son has seen you, too?" David asks. "As a dragon." Bronx looks exactly like his father. I remember when we met at the Rangers game.

I nod.

"And you're the reason why there are more dragons out in the city?" Manny's father, Daniel, asks. "We keep advising them to stay hidden, but some are not listening to us. Now that Regan is no longer Pride Leader, more and more dragons are doing their own thing. They are drawn to you and your magic."

"Yeah, about that," I say. "I was there when Regan died. It was on a Year Three mission. He told me that he knew the risks but needed to see for himself before he died. I think he knew he would be dying that night. When he was killed, I heard his voice in my head, and some of his magic absorbed into me."

"What did he say exactly?" Danzel asks.

"He said he needed to know if I was strong enough to

take his place. He died knowing that someday I would be, and the Pride would be in good hands."

"So, she's really not the Leader yet?" An older man with horn-rimmed glasses asks.

"She and the boys will be leaving tomorrow to find another PL to get training," Danzel says.

"I can hear the voices of the Pride, though," I say. "Ever since the night I was at the Slayers Council, I could hear them. Staten showed me how to block them out."

"It sounds like Regan wanted her to be Leader, and he gave her the connection."

"But she needs more," Daniel says. "She must have *the* magic, too."

"Maybe she does but can't unlock it?" David asks.

"That could be," Danzel says. "Staten has been working with her on her magic but hasn't indicated she has any barriers around her mind. It could the reason she's really gifted for her age."

"Unlock my magic?" I ask. "Is there something special about mine?"

"Brooklyn, Pride Leaders usually have very powerful magic running through them. It's what might allow them to hear the voices of their dragons, be able to protect them, call them when needed, and so much more. Which is why you need to find another PL."

"Danzel," David says. "Tell us more about the mission

you're sending her on."

"Staten came across a book that showed a dragon who has four companions, all seemingly connected to it. When he showed Brooklyn the image, she touched it and the picture came alive. He told me about it, and we think that Brooklyn is the one in the picture. The story behind it foretells of her coming and with her protectors, she will succeed in her mission."

"What is the mission it refers to?"

"That's the thing. It doesn't elaborate. I don't recall ever hearing any stories where a female dragon was prophesized, or what she's supposed to stop or save us or humans from."

More of the men shake their heads, also confirming that they don't know anything about the prophecy.

So my boys and I are going out on this mission blind? I thought it was just to become the Pride Leader. What else is going on here?

Chapter Twenty

The rest of the meeting is uneventful. Danzel recaps the Slayers Meeting information and while it is a very heated discussion, it is just that. They discuss options, and everyone seems to agree that they don't think the Slayers will hold the terms. Myself included. Allister agreed way too quickly on terms. He's planning something. Now to figure out what that is.

McQueen and I leave early as it doesn't seem that they need me there any longer. Danzel says it is just going to be boring administrative stuff that, as Leader, I won't be apprised of anyway. Those are the duties of a Second. It would have been nice to learn some of the goings on, but McQueen tugs me out the door. Danzel askes that we stay around the house just in case others wants to formally meet me or ask me more questions. So McQueen and I are lounging in the living room when the dining room doors open about fifteen minutes later.

"Excuse me." Someone taps my shoulder. I turn around and see the older gentleman with the horn-rimmed glasses speaking. "I'm Thom Fellows."

I stand from the chair and extend my hand. "Hello. I'm Brooklyn."

"It's a real pleasure to meet you, Miss. I didn't think in my lifetime I would ever meet a female dragon. It truly is an honor." He can't stop shaking my hand. I suppress a smile. He's super sweet and reminds me of my grandpa. "I was wondering something, though?"

"Yes?"

"It's not that I don't believe you. Especially, since the boys have vouched for you. But ..." He can't look at me.

"No. It's okay. I wouldn't believe it either if I hadn't actually shifted into a dragon. They told me I was one, and I didn't believe them." I bring forth my flames into an open palm and feel my magic slither across my arm. Green scales appear on my skin.

I watch as Mr. Fellows's eyes widen and then he gasps. The noise catches others in the room departing for the evening and they halt. They turn their gaze in my direction. Once they see the scales now running up my elbow and my claws, they press around me, hoping for a better view.

"Hey now," McQueen says. "Let's back up and give Brooklyn some space. She's not going anywhere, and you all can ask questions. But please step back. Remember, she's still new to magic and her dragon form. She doesn't always have control, and we don't want to see anyone get hurt tonight."

I nod my appreciation to him.

People allow me my personal space. Some want to touch my scales. Still others graze their fingers along my talons, as if to confirm that they are, indeed, real.

"Thank you, Brooklyn," Mr. Fellows says. "It's not that I didn't believe, but seeing it with my owns eyes banishes that slim doubt in my brain. Thank you for showing us."

A few more have questions about my parents, and I tell them they are not dragons, but they will help us if there is anything they can do. We think Allister won't trust them and won't include them on many items anymore. John Lorimer was also booted from meetings, so we lost our eyes and ears. But I tell them I'm working on something and will let them know by tomorrow evening one way or another.

Eventually, everyone clears the house except for Danzel and McQueen, leaving us to the living room again. "That went better than expected," Danzel says. "I was thinking that we'd never get anything said besides the proof."

"I think they've been waiting to see for themselves," McQueen says. "They've heard enough rumors, so many that they'd have to be true. Enough so that Regan died to see her."

"Yes, as sad as his death is for the Pride, I think you're correct, son." He turns to leave us. "Do you have everything ready for your trip?"

"We'll pack later tonight after we get back from flying." McQueen nods, asking me if that's still what I want to do this evening. I grin. "We'll be taking off here shortly, that is, if you don't need anything else from us, Dad?"

"No, you kids go on. I'll finish up with the meeting items. Have a good night."

"Thank you, Danzel," I say.

"Be safe out there."

"We will," McQueen says.

As soon as possible, McQueen and I are running out the back door. He's stripping out of his clothes as his feet hit the cement. I'm a bit more conservative, but I have already tugged my sweater over my head by the time my toes have the soft ground under them.

I shuck out of my pants, as my skin is morphing into a dragon. Scales appear faster than ever before, and I think it might be because for the last hour or so I've been surrounded by dragons. Powerful ones at that since they are on the Council.

By the time I catch a glimpse of McQueen, he's in his full form, and I'm a split second away from changing into mine. He doesn't look back to see where I am or how fast I'm shifting. He's taking flight into the sky, and I scurry after him.

We break over the invisible barrier, soaring in the night sky. The lights of New York are below us. My enhanced hearing can make out the hums of vehicles motoring along the streets. I can see the people milling about the sidewalks, going about their business, clueless to what beasts live among them.

We don't make it fifty yards when something buzzes past us. There shouldn't be anything up here. Birds know to stay away from us when we're in our dragon bodies. They can feel the predator within us. And we'd hear if a plane was near.

So what the heck was that?

"McQueen?" I ask.

"Yeah, I heard it." He sounds angry. "Don't know what it was."

"Maybe it'll circle back, and we can get another look at it?"

"Yeah."

"Any guesses?"

"No. It was too fast to see. It's like it was there and then gone."

"I know." Using my enhanced vision, I scan the skyline for anything that's out of place. "Are those planes over there?"

"Where?" His head turns in my direction.

"East, toward the school."

"Can't be. Too many of them close together."

"Should we take a closer look?"

"I don't know. I've got a bad feeling about it. So against my better judgement, yeah, we need to go see what those are." We soar higher into the sky. McQueen takes the lead, watching the horizon for anything amiss. *"Keep your ears open just in case a plane is this high up. Plane versus dragon isn't good for either of us."*

I do as I'm told and watch for airplanes. We glide closer to the blinking dots in the sky. We hear them, blades whirling. Then their outlines become visible.

They're drones. Flying around the city, hundreds of them.

"Who's controlling them?" I ask.

"Not sure. Could be a business, a school learning how to use them, or maybe even the government."

"Let's watch and see what kind of information they're gathering. And if an opportunity arises, take one down and reverse engineer it. Lock in the signal's location."

"And you've lost me."

"That's okay. I'm sort of a techy guy."

We both swoop down to get a closer look. Me, I'm staying farther back since I'm still new to flying and can't maneuver as fast nor as well as McQueen can. If we find ourselves in a bad situation, me not being able to handle myself while flying will not bode well.

With our eyes honed on the black drones darting around the city's landscape, we follow at a distance. They don't seem to be scanning for anything in particular. I do notice that they are in clusters of three or four, scouring the area for whatever it is they're searching for or supposed to be doing.

I think that's on purpose, for tactical reasons. If they are searching for dragons, we could take the hunk of junk out of the sky with one swoop from our claws. But if they are in a larger group and spread out, there's more of a chance that any one of them could send backup data or pictures to their home base if a few of them are destroyed. How did they create them in the first place if normal people can't see the dragons? If that were the case, then a regular security camera would have detected us years ago. Some sort of new technology infused with magic?

Great, now I'm thinking like them. But that's not a bad thing.

As McQueen nears a small grouping, they suddenly turn and emit a high-pitched beeping sound. Then a red laser fans out, scanning in front of them. His wings flap backward. He's too far back to collide with them, but we have no idea what the scan could mean.

"Let's get out of here," I say. *"See if they follow us."*

"Okay. There really isn't anything we can do while in our

dragon forms, but we can't go home. Not for a while anyway."

We bank right and head out toward the ocean, flying higher. Some of the drones do, in fact, follow us for a few miles but then return toward the city. None of them land, so we don't find out where their home base is. We'll have to keep watching the sky for them at night and during the day. And by we, I mean the other dragons who are not coming with me on my quest.

Chapter Twenty-One

McQueen and I fly across the Atlantic Ocean a few more hours, just to be certain none of the drones followed us this far out, and to make sure that none are spotted around his house. We take many resting stops since it is the first long distance flight for me and I'm not used to having wings.

We don't get a chance to practice fighting while in animal form, because my back hurts from the long flight. It's good, too, that I practiced flying for long distances.

By the time we land in the backyard, the house is dark, my body is sore, and I'm spent. McQueen, on the other hand, looks like he could go clubbing for another five hours.

I dress myself almost instantly. My magic courses through my body mid-shift, and as my skin is turning smooth, it's also being clothed. It's actually nice that I'm not naked for too long after each change. Not that McQueen or the boys have complained.

I catch McQueen spying on me as I pull my shoes on. I

flash him a wicked smile. He winks as he saunters toward me. His eyes roam up and down my body as that spark of awareness flares between us.

He holds out his hand and helps me up. His grip on my hand tightens. My eyes find his jade ones, and I think about kissing him. His lips part, and I know he's thinking the same thing.

"Are you ever going to kiss me again?" I bite my lip, drawing his attention where I want him to look. We continue to walk toward the house.

"You told me that next time you had to be the one who initiated it." He licks his lips. "I may be a cocky asshole, but when a woman says something like that, there's no messing around. I don't need to force myself." His gaze drops to my mouth. "Besides, eventually, you'd make the first move. I have every confidence in that. You wouldn't be able to keep your hands to yourself much longer."

"Oh, really?" I stop walking and place my hand on my hip, trying to be seductive.

"Yes."

"That sounds very much like a challenge."

He shrugs and keeps walking up the steps, opening the sliding glass door. He turns and flashes me his tongue ring.

Oh, boroughs. He knows exactly what he's doing.

Game on. Two can play at this game. I don't need him to kiss me. I'm seeing his brothers in the morning, and then we'll see who has the last laugh.

Without saying anything further, he stands in his doorway and watches me walk down the hall. I feel his eyes on me, so I do what I was pondering when I was outside.

I unbutton my shirt, showing my pink lace bra. I know he can see it even in the dark. My fingers fumble a bit with my pants button, but I manage to get it unclasped as I kick off my shoes. When I turn into my room, I drop them onto the floor and slide my pants down my thighs.

A low growl escapes from his throat.

I wink at him and then close my door.

The next morning, I still can't believe I did that in front of McQueen. It was so unlike me. I've never gone after a guy before. Manny and Bronx pursued me. And Staten, well … that sort of just happened.

I check my phone, and Noelle's text tells me that she'll be over within the hour. There's no need to meet at the coffee shop or send a vehicle because Manny is driving them.

He must have told her, or he's being the nice guy that he is and offered her a ride over here. I'm guessing it's the latter.

I get ready, pack for the trip, and head into the kitchen

for a late breakfast. Danzel and his wife, Eliza, are seated at the breakfast table quietly talking. Their heads are tilted toward each other, still in love. They remind me of my parents.

Boroughs, I miss them.

As quietly as I can, I shuffle back out, leaving them alone.

"You don't have to leave, Brooklyn," Danzel's deep voice says. "You're welcome to anything in the fridge. I know you kids got in early this morning, and you must be starving. I know McQueen usually is after being out in his dragon form for so long."

"Mr. Quee—"

"Danzel, I insist."

"We saw some drones out last night. Hundreds of them, and when we got close, some of them activated and did a scan of some sort. I don't think they hurt us. We know for sure they didn't follow us because we flew over the ocean for hours, just to make sure. I wanted to let you know in case we forgot and it's important."

"Thank you. I'll have someone look into it." He folds the newspaper. "You must have worn McQueen out with all that flying." He grins. "He's normally not the type to sleep in this late."

My face warms. "Um, yeah. By the time we got back in, he was pretty tired." I bury my head in the fridge and emerge with eggs and sausage. Opening various cabinets, I find a pan, but before I can reach for it, warm hands brush mine away.

"Good morning, Brooklyn," McQueen says.

"Morning. How did you sleep?"

He smiles. "Like a rock, actually."

"That's good to hear." I swallow. "May I have the pan?"

"Sure." He hands me it. "You going to make me breakfast, too?"

"Wasn't planning on it, but since you're here now, I can. I'm making eggs and sausage." Taking the egg container, I select six eggs and crack them into a bowl that McQueen hands me.

"I'll make the toast." He turns and removes a half loaf from a bread container.

"And we will leave you kids alone," Eliza says. She takes her husband's arm and walks out onto the patio.

"We didn't do anything last night," I say.

"I know that. You know that. But they are assuming we did because we're both acting weird."

"I'm not acting weird." I point to him. "You are."

The remainder of the time we prepare our food is in silence. Okay, maybe I am the one who's making this strange between us. It's not like we kissed last night. I might have wanted him to but he didn't. And I do have to say that he's being a gentleman about the whole thing if he's waiting for me to make the first move, especially after I did yell at him for stealing the first two kisses.

"I told your dad about the drones from last night." I take my plate to the kitchen table. "He's going to look into it while we're gone."

"Great."

We eat in continued silence. When we're done, we take our dinnerware to the sink, rinse, and stack them into the dishwasher. The electrical charge still zings between us, but neither of us says anything about it.

Chapter Twenty-Two

The doorbell rings. McQueen walks to the front door and opens it. Noelle launches herself into my arms "Hey, Brooklyn!"

"Hi, Noelle."

She looks around my arm and says, "Hi, McQueen."

"Hey, Darlin'. How you doing?"

We step apart. "Okay. Each day is getting better. You know?"

He nods. "Come on in."

"Manny is parking the car."

"I'll see if he needs any help."

I lead Noelle into the living room, taking a quick glance at her so I can see for myself that she is doing fine.

"How was the drive over?" I ask. "Were you guys followed?"

"I don't think so." Noelle sits on the couch.

I sit next to her. "So … um." My face scrunches, and my hands wring.

"Look. Just spit it out. I know you have something to say or ask me, which is why you had Manny bring me over this morning." She tilts her head. "Manny is here ... Bronx and Staten ... wait. They're going with you, someplace. Right? And that's why they're leaving."

Boroughs!

"Manny. McQueen? We might have a problem. Noelle guessed part of the reason why she's here and if she figured it out, then don't you think that Allister will, too?"

"That is a possibility," Manny says. *"If I were him, I'd keep eyes on all of us. But we've taken precautions. We drove around thirty minutes before we came here. We even stopped for coffee."*

"We'll be right in," McQueen says. *"I'm helping unload the rest of Manny's belongings from the trunk."*

"Noelle." I turn to face her. "Yes, you're correct. I'm leaving, and they're coming with me. We've lost our eyes and ears at the school, and I'm wondering if you'd—"

"Say no more. You want me to spy on the Council and report back to you?"

"I know it's putting you in a precarious situation, but we really need to know what's going on. The Council is meeting without my parents and John, and we think they are up to something."

"Okay, I'll do it."

I straighten. "Noelle, this is seriously life and death. If they catch you ... I don't want to even think what they'd do. But I can't see you hurt or killed. I won't. We've lost too many people already."

"I know. And that's why I need to do this. To help you guys. If the dragons want to live in peace, I want that for you guys. And if this helps accomplish that, then I'm in. Besides, there is something going on at the school. A small group of Third Years were taken out last night on a covert mission. Level Two's weren't invited to go scout, and no one spotted any dragons in the area, so I don't know what the mission was for."

Could it be that the Third Years are training on flying and controlling the drones? "Noelle," I say. "I need you to find out all the information on any secret missions anyone is being sent on, if Allister has any programs in the works that he hasn't unveiled yet."

Manny looks at me as he walks into the room. I smile back. "Hey, Brooklyn," he says. "If I were him, I would enable anything in the beta programs, to see if the slayers could get a leg up on any ambushes they coordinate against the dragons."

McQueen join us in the living room. "I'd also like to know what they're planning to use the drones for, if they can carry weapons, and where all the information is being stored. Think you can do that, Noelle?"

"What drones?" Noelle asks.

"Last night when we were out flying, we came across

them hovering around the city," I say. "It could be nothing. Could be something new the school is doing."

Noelle nods. "I'll try. These are the days I really wish I had magic, but I'll just have to depend on good old-fashioned investigating. Don't judge me for how I might have to accomplish it."

"No judgment from us," I say.

"Just don't compromise yourself or your morals, but we really do need that information," McQueen says. "We'll be leaving this afternoon, and I think it's best if we don't tell you where we're going just in case you are interrogated." Noelle nods. "But Brooklyn can still text you, so you know that she's okay. It might have to be in code in case Allister has found a way to track your phone or figures out who you're texting with."

"Let me change your name on my contact list." I pull out my cell and swipe the screen. Instead of the name Noelle under her phone number, I write Aunt Gertrude, showing her the name. "What are you going to write as mine?"

"Hmm … let me think." She taps her fingers on her knee. "How about this?" Quickly, she deletes my name and replaces it with: Little Brother. "Can you tell me what you're doing on your mission? Or is that top secret, too?"

I look at Manny and McQueen. From the looks on their faces, they would rather me not tell her. While that might be the better option, I don't like keeping secrets from my best friend. Thinking of Noelle's safety, I decide not to tell her the plan exactly. "I'll tell you when I get back."

What I don't tell her is that the Pride is leaderless, and the group is in disarray right now. Someone needs to fully submit to being the top of the organization, so everyone can fall into line. We don't need confusion within our ranks while we battle against the slayers, too.

And if what I suspect the drones are being used for is true, we're in for a big battle.

# Chapter Twenty-Three

It was nice to see Noelle, even if it was only for a short amount of time. I'd love to be there while she copes with Sax's death, but my mission is also important. We promise each other that we'll text soon but only for urgent news. McQueen has also suggested that we wipe our text history. He thinks that if either one of us is caught, we could say the other got a new phone number.

I find Manny in McQueen's room, unpacking and repacking into a single bag. From the looks of the room, Manny brought all of his school belongings in one trip. McQueen's bedroom is large enough to hold everything, but now it just makes it really cluttered. McQueen will have to reorganize more if Staten's and Bronx's things are coming over, too. I could offer my space to store some of their stuff. It's not like I'm going to be here.

"You all packed?" Manny asks when he notices me lingering in the doorway.

I nod. "Yes."

"Good."

"What are we going to do for money? I don't think we should use charge cards."

"I would agree," McQueen says as he walks out of his bathroom, holding toiletries in his hands. "I doubt the Slayers Council would go that far to hack into and track your credit card, but we will be careful and use cash whenever we can."

"All right, before we go to wherever we're going, I need to stop at the bank and pull out funds." I make room on the bed and sit. "Where are we going, anyway?"

"We'll head over to Europe since their Prides are older. Staten is meeting us at LaGuardia Airport, and Bronx will meet us in London."

"Why aren't we all going together?"

"Precautions, just in case we are followed. Once we get to London, we'll take a train, circle back, rent a car, and if we need to fly out again, we can."

That makes sense. It's like they've done this before. Me? This is my first time going on a covert operation and kinda on the run. I'm glad my boys will be there to protect me. I feel with my few days of training with McQueen, I've come a long way with techniques in my human and dragon forms.

We haul our luggage from the rooms and wait in the foyer of the house. Danzel called three different car rental places to have them all waiting here at the same time. McQueen's parents will be milling outside when we load into the various vehicles. We're each taking one on a different route and meeting at the airport.

I remind the boys that I'm stopping at the bank since I don't want to draw funds out at the airport. It's just another way to track us. Thanking his parents for allowing me to stay with them these past few days, I give my bag to the driver. I watch him load it into the trunk and can't help but think that maybe I forgot to pack something.

Manny is in the first vehicle, and McQueen takes the second. I hug each of my boys.

"I know it's only a few minutes, but I miss you guys already," I say. "Be careful and be safe." Giving them one more hug, we part.

"Don't worry, Brooklyn," Manny says. "Everything will be just fine. You'll be right behind us. I'll see you at the gate." He tugs me forward and kisses my lips, then steps back much too soon. "You'll be right behind us." He nods and climbs into the vehicle.

My face heats as I remember that McQueen's parents are standing out here with us.

"Be careful, Brooklyn," Danzel says. "Listen to the boys, or I should say, listen to Staten." He hugs me and then so does Eliza, then they head back inside the house.

Leaving me with McQueen. Do I kiss him? I know he

won't initiate it. But if something happens to us between here and getting to the airport, I'd never forgive myself. The current between us sparks, and my body automatically closes the distance. He's smirking at me. Maybe he knows this time I'm not bluffing. But something inside me, perhaps it's my dragon, tells me I can't let him walk away from me without showing him what he means to me.

"So, Babe, I should get going," he says. "You'll already be fifteen minutes behind us, and in case you run into anything and need to keep circling around blocks, to lose any tails, you'll be even later."

He is going to keep this all business and make me break first. Fine.

I step closer. "Thank you for training me this week. I'm glad that you're able to come with us." I place my palm on his chest. Even through his clothes, I can feel his heart beating. It's a steady rhythm but fast.

"You're welcome, Brooklyn." He takes a step back.

I step closer. "Yeah, so I'll see you in a bit."

He glances at me, then at my lips. Oh, boroughs, this is just stupid. I grab his shirt and pull him toward me. Our lips collide. I part his with my tongue. He opens and lets me in. My teeth hit his tongue ring. His hand caresses my face, keeping me locked against his mouth. My fingers dart into his soft hair. His other hand roams down my back.

Heat builds between us. I think my dragon even growls.

Or maybe that's me. But he, or his beast, answers my call. Our tongues still dance with each other as his hands explore my body.

A dog's bark from down the street finally gets us to break apart.

"Does this mean I can kiss you whenever now?" McQueen asks. "Because if that's still a no, then, Babe, you're going to be the death of me."

The car ride to the bank is short and uneventful. It gives me plenty of time to evaluate my actions, and what it means for me kissing McQueen like that. Sure, I like him. Under his brazen attitude, he really is a nice guy. And yes, I could see myself dating him. Would I give up Manny or Bronx or Staten? No. They are part of me, just as my arm is. There is no way that I'd even consider breaking up with either of them just to date McQueen. Besides, he is the one who pointed out that a woman these days doesn't have to choose and can date multiple guys. Just like the Bachelorette.

I stash the wad of cash into my purse. My magic flares, and it makes me think that I'm missing something. Did I forget to pack an item? We don't know how long we'll be gone and whatever it is, I may not be able to buy it where we're going. Checking the time, I still have plenty of time to swing back to McQueen's house and take one more look and then get to the airport. I know I told the guys I'd go to the bank and then directly to the airport, but I can't stop this niggling feeling that I need to go back to my bedroom.

I tap the driver before I can change my mind. "Could you swing me back to the house?" I ask. "I forgot something."

He nods, turning right on the next street and circling back toward the river.

I check my purse one more time, confirming that my driver's license, passport, and money are securely in my travel wallet. I have one credit card for emergencies since all of that can be tracked, but it might be needed for booking plane and car rentals. I'm pretty sure that bus and train stations take cash. And if we're really in a crunch, we can use our thumbs.

A flash of light takes my attention away from checking my belongings. I lean my head on the window and look to where I thought the flash was. I don't see anything out of place. Turning around, I check the back window for anything in the sky. I don't realize I'm looking for drones until the driver says something.

"I didn't think people could have those blasted things hovering so low toward the ground," he says. "Every day, I see more and more of them. They're becoming a menace."

I duck down in hopes that they haven't seen me.

What are they doing out now? And who's controlling them? It's almost like they are getting the lay of the land. None of them emit any laser, like last night's ones. But that doesn't mean they can't. Nor does it mean these are the same ones. The ones at night could be constructed for night flying, where these have a different purpose.

It doesn't take long before the car is parked outside McQueen's house. Even though his parents keep saying that this is my house, I feel awkward walking right into it. So instead, I decide to ring the front doorbell.

Eliza opens the door. "Oh, Brooklyn. Did you forget something?" she asks.

"Yeah, I think I did, so I just need to run and grab it." I brush past her as she glides out of my way and run down the stairs into my room. Quickly, my eyes dart around.

Then they land on the blue jewelry boxes. My magic pulses to life again, and it draws me toward them. What would I need my jewelry for on a mission like this? Should I bring them?

I turn my back and walk toward the closet, but my flames appear on my fingers. That's never happened before. I look down at the tips, and they burn bright green. The flames flicker back toward the dresser, as if a wind is coaxing them to draw me down the path.

Standing in front of the boxes, I lift my hands and the fire extinguishes. Okay, if I'm supposed to bring them with, then I better.

To save space in my small purse, I remove each piece from its container and combine them into the necklace box. I swing the shoulder strap across my body and secure my most precious items.

Chapter Twenty-Four

The airport is loud and bustling with travelers. I easily slip into a crowd and follow them to the security checkpoint. The wait isn't too long since I have TSA Pre-Check on my boarding pass, and then I go and find my gate, wheeling my small suitcase behind me.

I opted not to take any of the pieces from the Louis Vuitton set, so I woudn't draw attention to myself. Instead, it's a black roller bag that I borrowed from McQueen.

I easily spot three of my boys standing near the window, their backs turned to me, giving me ample time to admire their backsides. Oh, and yes, their broad shoulders and tapered waists.

As if they know I'm watching them, they turn as one. Each acknowledges me in their own way. Manny waves, walking in my direction. Staten nods his hello and follows Manny. McQueen just grins and stays where he is. He knows eventually I'll make my way to him, smug bastard that he is.

Manny reaches me first. "How was your ride over?" he asks. "Uneventful like all of ours was?" He places a light kiss on my cheek. I'm sure that the people around us think that he and I are the couple.

Staten doesn't try to show me any physical affection. I don't expect him to, though. Plus, I don't want to make it awkward for him, now that we're out in public.

"No one was trailing us, if that's what you mean," I say. "But my driver said that he's been seeing more drones out, and they're flying lower than they're supposed to." We walk toward the window where McQueen is leaning against it, watching us. "He didn't know anything else about it. Didn't seem to really care but said that they are a nuisance."

"Hey, Babe." McQueen takes my bag and leans in for a kiss. There are too many people waiting at the gate, and I'm sure that none of them saw Manny kiss me earlier. Normally, I would have blushed about it. But that's a thing of the past. "My parents texted and said you stopped at the house. Did you forget something?"

"Yeah, but it's all good now." I pat my purse. "Has anyone been in contact with Bronx? He knows where we're going?"

"Yes," Manny says. "Staten told him yesterday and again this morning. He's meeting us at the London Eye. It's a tourist trap and should have lots of people."

I nod. "And has a spectacular view of the city and the Thames River." I lower my voice. "What's the plan once we get there, and Bronx is with us? I just hate this not knowing where we're going."

Staten comes to stand in front of me, forming a tight circle with our bodies, blocking the view from everyone. "We'll take the train to Holyhead and then catch the ferry to Dublin," he says. "We haven't pre-booked anything, so we'll use cash along the way. Once we get to Ireland, we'll grab a couple of cabs and travel to Phoenix Park. We'll take a look around the area, but I'm sure we'll have to come back later at night when the dragons are out. Dad also said that the Farmleigh House is used for their Pride, but we can't just walk in. We need to be invited to stay there. Until that happens, we'll be staying at the Phoenix Park Hotel."

I nod. That sounds like a good start. I point to the chairs and the circle breaks, allowing me through.

After taking a few steps, my stomach cramps, and I almost keel over. Luckily, Staten is right there and snatches my elbow, preventing me from doing a face plant. I hold my arms around my waist to comfort the off-putting feeling. My magic flares, but I squash that almost immediately. I'm not fast enough though; I can see Staten's come to life, too.

Then my side hurts. My hand splays on my ribs. Pain shoots up the right side of my body. I'm bending over in

Staten's strong arms. He's trying to usher me to the chairs without calling more attention to us. Eventually, he picks me up and sets me down after someone sees us and moves.

"What's wrong?" Staten asks. "You're pale. You don't look so hot." His brothers give him a slap on the head. "What was that for?"

"Move over lady charmer," McQueen says. "Babe, tell me what hurts. What are you feeling?"

I can barely get any words out. My mouth is dry and gritty. Muscles I didn't know I had scream at me, even though I'm just sitting here. "I don't know what's wrong." I exhale. "It's like it's me but not me. I don't know how to explain it."

"Is she okay?" A voice I've never heard asks. I'm staring at a pair of navy women's shoes. I tilt my eyes up. A gate checker stands in front of me. "Are you okay, Miss?" she asks again.

I lift my head up and straighten in the chair. The last thing we need is for me to go to the hospital or the airport medical facility. "Yeah, I'm fine. I just ... think I ate something that didn't agree with me."

"All right. Take it easy." She points over my left shoulder. "The women's restrooms are that way. Maybe one of these guys can help you."

I nod. "Thank you." I watch her walk away and return to the podium. "I don't really need to go, so you guys can stop thinking about who should take me."

"Seriously, though, Brooklyn," Manny says. "What's wrong?"

"I honestly don't know, but right now, I feel like myself again. Nothing hurts. Could it be because of ..." I flick my fingers to show them my magic, so I don't have to say the words.

"I guess it could be," Staten says. "We'll keep an eye on you, but you tell us if you feel that way again."

An announcement comes on and informs the waiting passengers that Flight 0424 will be boarding soon.

"I think I will go to the restroom and freshen up before we get on the plane." Manny stands, but I wave him away. "I can go by myself. But thank you." I kiss him on the lips and then depart.

I walk toward the bathroom, thinking cold water on my face will wash away the horrible lingering feeling. I turn the faucet on. My reflection is terrible looking. Pulling out a brush, I run it through my long hair and then apply a bit of eyeliner and shadow. Lastly, I glide lip gloss on my lips and pucker. It's the best that I can do with the small amount of makeup I packed with me.

My fingers brush along the jewelry box. I hesitate. I brought them with, made a special trip back to the house for them. I should wear them. Poking the earrings through the hole in my lobes, I turn my head from side to side. They dangle to my chin and make a small clanking sound. Then I clasp the necklace around my neck. Slipping the ring onto my right hand, I spread my fingers to watch the gems sparkle. Finally, I add the bracelet.

I think that all of the boys will appreciate seeing them on me.

Chapter Twenty-five

It's been a long time since I've flown on a commercial airline. I'm glad I don't have to sit next to strangers. Once we all board the plane, I'm sandwiched between Manny and McQueen. Staten is sitting across the aisle from us. No one said anything about my added jewelry, probably because my hair is covering it. I pull my earbuds out and settle in for the long flight.

I catch Staten gazing at me. He taps his ear and smiles. I return his smile and mouth, "thank you." He adjusts his position and closes his eyes.

Manny looks at his Staten, then to me. He takes my hand and holds it. I lean into him and relax. He flips my wrist to look at the ring, then his eyes raise to the base of my neck. A smile stretches across his face.

McQueen pats my knee, then pulls out a couple of magazines from his backpack and starts flipping through the pages.

As far as international flights go, it isn't too bad. After

listening to music most of the way, napping and chatting with Manny and McQueen, the seven-hour long flight passes in a flash. Before long, we are debarking the plane with our luggage in tow.

The airport is just as busy as LaGuardia as we snake our way to the street level to grab some taxis to take us to the London Eye, where Bronx is meeting us.

My stomach churns the closer we get to the gigantic Ferris wheel overlooking the Thames River. At first I brush it off as nerves from the flight and the impending mission of finding another Pride Leader. But as we make our final approach over the Waterloo Bridge, I realize it has to be something else.

I watch Staten check his phone again. He's not worried, nor has he said that he is. I don't even know if he, or if any of the boys, has tried to mentally contact their brother. Catching Staten's eyes, I tilt my head in question. Without verbalizing it, he knows what I'm asking and shakes his head.

Manny squeezes my hand, a reassuring gesture.

"We have some time to kill before Bronx's flight arrives," Staten says. "If you guys are up to it, we can take in some sights."

I've been to London on many occasions, but each time there is something new I see or a place I've never been to. We decide to hang around the area. "How about visiting the London Dungeon?" I ask. "Then we can go to the Aquarium. If there's more time, the Florence Nightingale Museum is nearby, too."

"Sounds good to me, Babe. We've never been to this city before. Manny, have you?"

"Nope. Never had the chance to go abroad."

"Okay," I say. "A zoo is a zoo, so perhaps we can skip that. I think you guys might enjoy the Imperial War Museum instead. It's farther away but still doable to walk there."

We pay cash for the hour-long tour around the grounds and inside the dungeons. The boys are fascinated with the history and, of course, the weapons like a real guillotine. I know from their expressions that they'll love the weapons museum.

Since it's a beautiful early evening and it took us seven hours during the day to get here, we opt to take the sidewalks and walk to the next tourist trap.

Of course, as soon as the double cannons sitting in front of the building come into view, I can feel the excitement emitting from the boys. Again, we pay cash and walk around the building on a self-guided tour, taking in various vehicles used over the centuries: artillery weapons, fighter planes, and boats.

The boys walk around like kids in a toy store, wanting to touch everything. Of course, there aren't too many things that can be, since most historical items are kept behind plexiglass or suspended in the air.

Staten checks the time again. It's been three hours since we landed, and we should get back to the rendezvous point.

My head spins, and I lose my balance again. McQueen is there this time to help me. "What's wrong?" he asks. "Is this like what happened at the airport?"

I nod. "Yes, but it's not as bad as before." I don't know how I know, but Bronx is not going to be waiting for us at the Eye.

"Let's get you outside," Staten says. "Maybe some fresh air will help."

I don't have the heart to tell him that it won't. But we leave the museum and head to a secluded park bench. The boys shield me with their bodies.

"Try using your magic and tell me what you feel," Staten says.

I do as Staten suggests. Carefully, I bring my flames to my opened palm, letting the energy travel throughout my body. It swirls and hums, locking onto the tiny part that's Bronx. The connection I feel with him is alive but fluttering. Hmm, that's never happened before. Is he in trouble?

He told me once we're connected. He gave me a part of his soul. And that's what I find—a bright, emerald green spark of everything that he's made of. The goodness in his heart. The sureness of himself. His love for me and his brothers.

"Bronx?" I mentally ask him. I'm pretty sure that Staten has already tried communicating with him, but I need to do it for myself. *"Hey, can you hear me?"*

I don't get a response, but I do caress the bond between us in case he can feel me, so he knows I'm thinking of him.

"I can't help think that my fatigue has to do with Bronx," I say. "There's something wrong. I've tried contacting him through our bond but nothing." I stand and start walking toward the Eye. Maybe he's there already.

"I haven't been able to connect with him either," Staten says. "And I've been trying all day."

"I'm worried about him."

"He's a big boy and can take care of himself," McQueen says.

"What if he was taken?" Manny asks. "He might not be able to fend off everyone. I know he doesn't like killing humans, or dragons for that matter."

"Look. Let's not speculate on anything." Staten shakes his head. "It's just going to drive us crazy creating all sorts of what ifs. When we know something solid, we can address it." He turns to his brother. "Call Dad and see if he's heard anything about Bronx. Brooklyn, call Noelle and see if she's seen him at the school. And if not, have her go casually look for him."

It doesn't take too long to walk the few blocks to get back to the river. We linger around the meeting spot and as time passes, the sinking feeling in my chest about Bronx becomes greater.

McQueen talks with his dad, but Danzel doesn't have any news on Bronx. He didn't know he was missing. He said that he'd get one of the techies to see if Bronx actually boarded his flight.

I contacted Noelle, leaving a voicemail for her to call me as soon as she gets my message. I also leave her a coded text.

Me: Have you seen my friend? We're supposed to be meeting soon, and I haven't heard anything. Getting worried.

We wait around for another couple of hours, watching the tourists come and go. We gaze at the boats driving along the river into the sunset. I watch the Eye go around in circles. And we wait.

Chapter Twenty-Six

Eventually when the moon is high in the sky, my own eyes feel like sand is caked under the lids, and I can no longer feel my legs from standing so much, Staten suggests that we stay in a hotel close by just in case Bronx's flight had some issues. We've all used our phones throughout the evening, researching his flight in case something happened to it. All of our batteries are running on empty, just like we are.

As we tote our bags with us, Staten checks us into the Park Plaza Westminster Bridge Hotel, across from the Waterloo Station. There, we get a one-room suite with two beds; it's all they have left. Thankfully, the hotel clerk didn't ask if we are celebrating anything special. Perhaps the lady thought we are brothers and sister traveling together.

When we finally get into the room, I flop onto the bed while the boys plug in their phones.

I try once again to reach Bronx in my mind. *"Please*

answer me if you can. Everyone is getting really worried about you."

Manny orders us room service while McQueen is in the shower. I'm still lying on the bed when I feel it dip. From the sandalwood smell, I know it's Staten. "Hey, Brooklyn." I sit up. "We'll find him."

"I know. My mind is running with worst case scenarios, which isn't helping."

"We all are. I understand. Try to get some sleep. If he doesn't arrive tomorrow, we still need to press on to Ireland. Dad will let us know if a trail is picked up on him. Then we'll hurry back if need be. I won't let my brother die at the hands of the enemy. Not if I can help it. But right now, we don't know who has him, if anyone does."

"I know," I say again.

Manny and McQueen join us in the bedroom when my phone vibrates. Picking it up, I swipe it on, and it's a text from Noelle.

Noelle: Sorry, had a mission. Back now. No excitement from that. Let me check on your friend. Give me 30.

The wait is excruciating, but thankfully our food arrives and gives us something to do while Noelle goes and looks for Bronx. I wonder what she's going to tell us about the mission and if she's found anything about the drones.

Finally, my phone rings. I grab it with shaking hands.

161

Manny gently takes it from my fingers and answers for me. "Noelle, this is Manny," he says. "You're on speaker. Go ahead."

"Hey, guys. I assume that everyone is with my girl?"

"Yes, we're all here," I say. "Except for Bronx."

"Yeah, about that. He's not at the school. I didn't want to ask a whole lot of people. I know a couple of students who have him as an instructor for the last class of the day, and they said his class was cancelled. No one has seen him. I swung by the Lounge, the training center, and his room. That's where it gets interesting."

I cringe. Manny drapes his arm around my shoulders.

Noelle continues, "His room was unlocked, and the door slightly opened. So I pushed it all the way, so I could see if he was in there. It looked like his room was broken into."

"This is Staten. How do you mean? What did his room look like?"

"I've never been in his room, but things were thrown about. Drawers were opened, and others were lying on the floor. Most of his clothes were gone, but I expected that since he was packing it all up to leave. But the desk lamp was broken, and the bed turned on its side. It kinda looked like there was a struggle in there."

"Shit!" McQueen says.

"Yeah," Manny agrees.

"Okay," Staten says. "Thanks, Noelle, for looking into it. I think it's safe to assume that he was taken by force. My bet is a Slayer Team because the dragons wouldn't do that. Even the rogues wouldn't use him to get to Brooklyn."

"Why is that?" I ask.

"Because they would have the entire Pride rain down on them. While they are rule breakers, they don't need a price on their heads. It just makes more sense that it's the Slayers who have him," Staten explains.

"Noelle?"

"Yeah?"

"We'll catch a flight out tomorrow or the next day and come home to look for him." I don't ask Staten if that's what we plan to do. I'm not taking no for an answer. There is no way I'm letting Bronx be where he is for another day. Not if I can help it. Besides, they could be torturing him. "We need to stop at a place first and then catch a ride home. In the meantime, have you looked into the drones?"

"Oh, yeah. I asked one of the Third Years about it. Don't ask any questions about how I got the answers. Anyway, he said that Mr. Astor pulled the best candidates from that Level and is training them on how to use them. Each drone is equipped with specialized scanning lasers searching for dragons in the sky. It's a new technology that's been years in the making. Taking magic and infusing it with mechanics. Those can be day or night drones. Some have titanium tracking darts that fire if they identify a dragon. All information is being captured and downloaded into a server room someplace on campus. The guy didn't know where. But they are teaching the students how to fly them and how to fire the darts. They've set up a schedule, and there are at least a dozen drones out at any given time."

We let her talk and give us the entire story. It's unbelievable. "Noelle?" I ask. "Try to get some information on the darts: what they do, can they kill, are they a sedative. What's the end game of using the drones? Are they trying to capture a dragon?"

"Yeah. Okay. I'll go back to the guy. It might take a few days, though. Most of Level Three has stopped training and are in the drone rotation."

"Good work, Noelle," Staten says. "Keep us posted, and we'll see you in a few days." After a moment of silence, he nods at me.

"Okay, it's really late here, so we're going to bed," I say. "Thanks, Noelle."

"Night everyone. Sleep well." She giggles and cuts the connection.

Oh, boroughs. We have our work cut out for us now. Not only do we still have to find a Pride Leader willing to help me, but we also have to find Bronx and get him back to us in one piece. The start of this mission is already going to shit.

Chapter Twenty-Seven

I can't say for sure if the boys got any sleep. What I can tell you is we all look like hell the next morning. By the dark circles under our eyes and the rumpled clothes we still wear, it was a sleepless night for everyone.

I know we're thinking of Bronx and are running through a melee of questions in our minds. Questions that no one wants to ask out loud for fear that those possibilities will come true if voiced.

We order breakfast as we rotate in the bathroom and get ready for the day. Staten is firm that we still need to travel to Ireland today to see if their leader will meet and work with me. Since we came all the way over here, we can't turn back empty-handed. Bronx wouldn't want us to.

Our phones are fully charged and while I'm in the shower, Manny is looking up train schedules to get us to the ferry.

I'm the last to use the bathroom, but I don't dawdle. I've checked the map and know that it'll take quite a few hours to get to Holyhead by train. Running my hands through my wet hair, I emerge from the room and smell hot bacon and eggs waiting for me. Again, I'm wearing Staten's earrings and when he notices them, he smiles. Man, I love seeing those dimples. My heart aches a little more each time I see them.

"It's about six hours to the ferry," Manny says. "We'll need to take a taxi, and soon, if we're going to make the 8:45 train."

I nod as I shovel food into my mouth. McQueen and Staten pack their stuff. Manny's bag is already sitting at the door. Before long, I'm packed, and we check out of the hotel. We make our way to the Euston Station to catch the train that'll take us to Holyhead ferry.

"Bronx?" I'm not giving up on him. I keep telling myself that maybe it'll be the next time that I hear him through the bond.

The crew is quiet this morning, each lost in our own thoughts. Staten buys us tickets, and we're running to board the train. We find an open cabin and claim it as our own. Maybe some of us can get some sleep during this part of the journey. McQueen sits next to me and tells me to lean against him and sleep, which I fight. But the constant lull of the train and the smooth rhythm as it glides on the tracks forces my eyes to close.

"I've been waiting for you, Brooklyn."

My eyes snap open. I'm in my dragon form, back on the plateau overlooking the mountain landscape. A green dragon is hovering in front of me.

"Bronx?"

"Yes, Sweetheart. It's me. You're finally asleep and in a calm enough state for me to bring you here. Where are you guys?"

"Where are you? No one can get ahold of you. We're worried sick." I watch as his wings fold, and he lands next to me on the ledge. *"Tell me everything you know, so we can come get you."*

"I don't know where I am. All I know is that one minute I was in my room packing, and then four guys come charging in. I fought them the best I could. I think I broke one guy's ribs, but they still overpowered me. Gave me a shot of something because the next thing I knew, I woke up in a cell of some sort. No windows, just cement blocks. It's musty, so I think I'm underground."

I rub my head against his chest. It's so good to feel him, to know at least in this dream he's safe. My dragon must feel the same way. She's purring.

"We're on our way to Ireland today looking for their Pride Leader, and after that we're coming home to find you. Staten says that since we're over here we might as well try him since we didn't have any leads on you. But now—"

"No. You guys continue on that path. I'm not going anywhere." Bronx nuzzles me back.

"But they could kill you."

"And what good would that be? They need me alive to get you. They want you, Brooklyn. You're the only one they know who is a dragon. They think you'll lead them to the rest of us."

"So they don't know you are one?"

"No. At least I don't think so."

"When we land, I'm going to use our bond to find you."

"It might not work. I think they're drugging me or something. This is the first time I'm coherent enough to try contacting you."

I clench my jaw. *"If they hurt you, so help me God."* My dragon agrees; a rumbling sound comes from deep within my throat. *"It could be in the food or drink. They are giving you at least that, right?"*

"Yes. Bread and water."

I nod. *"Try to hold out for a couple of days. We need the connection to be open. We'll fly out of Ireland as soon as we can. Maybe gauge it to stop eating in two days. Since we're seven hours ahead of New York, I'm assuming that's where you're being kept."*

"It's logical, but again, I don't know."

I feel Bronx begin to fade and then watch his dragon disappear. *"Bronx, don't go. Not yet!"*

"I can't stop it, Sweetheart. I'm sorry. I must be waking up. I'll eat for a few days and then stop. Hopefully, that'll give you time ...

I jolt awake. "Bronx!" I sit up.

"It's okay, Babe," McQueen says. "I've got you. It was only a dream."

"I saw Bronx. He's okay. Someone took him. They're holding him in a cell. I told him to give us two days to get to him."

"What else did he say?" Staten leans in closer, putting his elbows on his knees.

"Four guys jumped him in his room. He thinks he broke one of their ribs." I watch Staten pull out his phone and text someone. "They're feeding him bread and water. That's all I know."

"I just texted Dad to look into the hospitals for any man with broken ribs brought in the last twenty-four hours. If he finds one, he'll get there and interrogate him. He could be one of the kidnappers. I've also asked him to look into the why and possible locations. This could be an act of war if the slayers have him."

Smart. And that's why Staten is the self-imposed leader of the group.

A knock on the cabin door startles me. Through the frosted glass, a person's body can be seen. Manny stands and glides open the door. "Yes?"

"Lunch is being served in the dining car if you'd like to buy anything," a train worker says.

"Thank you." Manny closes the door and turns to us. "Food, anyone?"

"You know I'll always eat," McQueen says.

I adjust my clothes and run fingers through my hair, standing. "I'm ready."

Throughout lunch and the rest of the train ride, the boys chat while I remain relatively quiet. I chime in every now and then but leave them to their conversation. My dream with Bronx has soothed me. At least he's okay.

Boroughs. I didn't even ask him if he was hurt. He better not be, or I'll be going full dragon and smashing his captors to bits when I find them.

Chapter Twenty-Eight

I manage to get another short nap in before we disembark the train. The ticketing line is short, and again Staten buys our passes. There is a ferry leaving in ten minutes. The two-hour ride across the Irish Sea will be a welcome change from being cooped up in the cabin.

We won't see the sunset, but I can imagine what it would look like from the superferry. Ideally, all of my boys would be with me, and we'd watch from the highest deck. For now, I'm surrounded only by three of them. We decide to hang out on the decks, warm our faces from the sun, and feel the wind blow through our hair. It's like flying, but slowly across the open sky.

After the ferry ties to the dock, we take our belongings, hail a cab, and ride the eight miles to Phoenix Park Hotel. We check into the room and opt to sleep in the same room once more. Plus, it saves on costs.

We freshen up and change into more durable clothes. I opt to wear my specially made duster jacket, shirt, and black jeans. I didn't pack the boots, so my sneakers will have to do.

McQueen suggests that we sit down and eat as we wait for dusk. As we meander the streets, we spot Ryan's F.X. Buckley, a steak restaurant. Of course, we order rare or medium-rare steaks, which I understand since we're dragons. The interior is nicely lit with green hanging lights. Blue striped wallpaper that reminds me of a pinstriped shirt hides the endless bottles of wine as the chalk boards show the daily menu.

After our food comes out, I ask to no one in particular, "Are we going to walk the park and see who's out? Will they be in dragon forms, or how will we know they are one if they appear as humans?"

"You'll be able to *see* some part of their dragon form while as a human," Staten says. "Send a bit of magic into your eyes when we're out. Most dragons over here wear their scales as a second layer of skin all the time, so transformations are quick." He looks at McQueen. "He tells me that you're getting really good at shifting, almost as fast as us. Keep practicing, and you'll get it. McQueen also said that you've mastered changing into clothes halfway through shifting so when it's done, you're not naked. That part you taught yourself."

"Yep, sure did. I was experimenting with magic and just thought of it, so I tried."

"Sorry, I didn't even think to train you on that. Since we're all males, it never occurred to me." Staten presses his lips in a thin line.

"It's okay. I know how now."

We eat our dinner and then head out of the restaurant. The sun is setting, splashing dark blue and purple waves in the sky. The short walk to the park entrance gives me an uneasy feeling. The farther we head on the road that cuts through the property, I notice that the lawn is groomed, the shrubs are trimmed, and tall trees line the streets. The park is well cared for.

Taking a left off the main street, we run across the sports grounds and past a building. We press up against a dense thicket.

"Brooklyn, no matter what happens tonight, stay close to one of us," Staten says. "Do as you're told, so we can worry less about you."

"I don't need codd—"

He holds up his hand. "Call your magic up, and keep it hovering all over your body, pressing it against yourself, so it's ready in case you need to change. I'll lead. Manny and McQueen, take her sides. We'll stay in human form as long as we can, so we're not showing aggression toward them."

"If it comes to fighting," I say. "I'm not sitting it out. I won't have you guys die for me."

"Babe." McQueen squeezes my hand. "It's what we are. We are your protectors, and we need to keep you safe."

"That does not mean you have to die for me. It doesn't mean that you do all the fighting for me. I'm not a child. I may not be able to change as fast as you guys, and I may not be able to kill another dragon, but I'm bigger than most others I've seen, so I can use my body weight."

Manny's mouth opens but I stop him. "I'm not done." He smirks. "If I'm to really become the Pride Leader, then I have to be willing to take risks for the whole group. That doesn't mean putting you in front of me all the time. I will be next to you. Treat me as an equal. That's all I'm asking."

"I was just going to tell you," Manny finally says. "That you are wearing the earrings that Staten gave you and the necklace I gave you for your birthday, and that you'll want to keep them safe."

I drop my eyes, "Ah, thanks." So he had noticed but didn't say anything about them. I twirl the ring on my right hand, thinking of keeping it safe for Bronx, so he can see me wearing it the next time we see each other.

After my little rant, we continue forward in the dark. The trees hide our shadows and without any city and streetlights, there is only the moon and the stars out to guide us to our destination. I have no idea where that is, so I'm following behind Staten.

As we make our way, up ahead on a small hill stands a

cross. It soars high into the sky. The white stone, or whatever material it's made from, has no lights highlighting it.

The park has long since closed as we climb the hill to the base of the monument. From up here, we can see for miles in all directions. I bet on a clear, sunny day, it's even farther. On the opposite side is a staircase leading to parking lots. It's lined with trees and a forest behind that.

My boys tense but don't grab for any of their hidden weapons. Peaceful contact is what Staten said. They scan the area, making me become alert and look for any strangers in our midst.

And then we see them, stalking out of the tree line. Five dragons. From this distance, I can't tell their coloring. Their heads are held high. There could be more behind them.

As large as they are, they don't make any sounds. If I hadn't seen them with my own eyes, I wouldn't have known them to be in the park with us. They continue to advance, and we hold our ground. Could they communicate with us since we're from different Prides?

The center one keeps walking while the four flanking his sides stop. The dragon before us is varying shades of blue. His black eyes roam over each of my companions. His head angles to see me better since I'm still stuck behind Staten and sandwiched between Manny and McQueen.

I shove my way through them, taking two steps

forward. The dragon growls. My boys answer with their own loud snarls, which in turns sparks the rest of them to do the same.

"Stop it," I say. "I'm guessing that you can understand me, so you'll need to show me a sign." I point to myself. "I'm Brooklyn Bryer, and I've come to see your Leader." The blue dragon nods his head. "You will take me to him, along with safe passage for me and my protectors." I wave to my boys. The dragon shakes his head as loud rumbling sounds emit from him. His wings extend and flap. "I don't mean you or the Pride harm. I just need to speak to your Leader."

"It'd be easier if they shifted to human form, so we're not having this one-sided discussion," Staten says.

"I know, but I understand why they aren't." Turning back to the beast in front of us, I say, "We're from New York's Pride." He nods. "And it's imperative that I get guidance from your Leader. He needs to teach me or show me how to command the Pride."

The rest of the dragons rustle their wings. They must not like what I said. Perhaps they think I'm a human who wants to be in charge of all dragons. Should I show them? It might put them at ease.

Magic hums around us. It's strong, more potent than I've felt in a long time. It's old and strange, but not. The snout and jaw we've been looking at morphs into a human mouth, but everything else remains the dragon. That's good to know that I might be able to do that, too.

"What are you?" he asks.

"We are dragons," Staten says.

"I know you three are, but what is she?"

"I'm a dragon," I say.

"There is no such thing."

Our focus has been on the animal standing before us, so we didn't see some of the others follow suit. They look strange with human lips.

"Trickery or something," someone shouts.

"No, I swear it's not a trick. I'll prove it."

Before my boys can stop me, I take a step forward and let my magic take me. I've had it out and on the ready since we walked into the park. The shift is almost instant.

The Irish dragons back up. Some take to the sky. But the blue one holds his ground and rears up. Smoke blows out from his nose.

I hear my boys change. They answer with their own billowing smoke.

And then it begins. Exactly what we didn't want to happen.

Chapter Twenty-Nine

The five Irish dragons charge us, three from the ground and two from the sky.

Staten meets the aerial attack while we take on the rest. Despite all my big words from earlier, I'm scared shitless. This is real. This is life and death. My boys could die. I could die.

I wish Bronx were here. Not to die with us, but to even the odds. He's a great fighter, and I'm lucky to have him in my corner. But I can't think of him right now. I need to focus on what's happening in front of me.

Manny and McQueen charge the blue dragon since he's the immediate threat. I leave them to it so I'm not distracting them or getting in the way. Instead, I let the two others come to me. I lead them away to give us room to maneuver.

I'm a head and neck taller than my opponents. I remember my training with McQueen about using my height and weight as the advantage over more experienced fighters. I'm not as quick as they are. My large tail swings back and forth, and my black leathery wings expand, trying to make me look as threatening as possible.

I fill my chest with the building heat. Once they come near, I'll unleash fire. It doesn't take long for them to be in range. I shoot fire toward them. They dodge it easily, as if they're ready for it. I won't be the needy girlfriend who needs saving, at least not yet. But I don't want to kill these guys.

I have no idea how Staten is faring with his two foes, nor how Manny and McQueen are doing against the blue dragon. The two I'm battling are trying to corral me. I remember what happened last time I was herded. My dragon didn't like it. I didn't know anything back then, and I won't be sidelined now if I can at least hold my own.

I spare a glance at my boys, even though I know exactly where they are because of our connection. They look to be okay. They aren't dead, so that's a plus.

The cream and the lavender dragons don't need to come to me. I rush the purple one on my right, catching him off guard while I throw all of my weight into his chest. He stumbles and goes down. I roll so I don't face-plant, using the momentum to spring back onto my legs. I'm ready for the cream-colored one as he charges me. I slam my tail into his legs. He leaps over it and doesn't expect my neck to be so long as I'm curled into a tight ball. My teeth graze his wings, shredding them.

A horrific screech fills the night.

I don't let up. As sad as it makes me seeing another dragon in pain, I snap at his neck. Using my claws, I scratch along his body. Blood pools around us, making the ground slippery. I'm so focused on the animal on the ground that suddenly, I'm thrown off balance.

I'm exactly where I don't ever want to be: beneath a dragon baring his teeth against my neck.

My magic builds again. It's flickering since I'm so scared. This is it. I barely made it out of my teenage years. I've been the Pride Leader for all of a couple of days, but I've experienced love on a level so deep that I'm glad I have my boys. All of them.

He's pulling his head back, jaws opening, ready to make the kill.

"Brooklyn!" Manny screams. "Get up! Don't stop fighting. We're coming."

A different kind of burn starts in my heart and courses throughout my body. Bright green magic glows on my scales. It's pulsing, building.

"Babe, fight. Remember what I taught you."

It all happens so fast. I hear my boys in my mind. I see them coming toward me. They are bringing the three others with them.

"Be who you are meant to be," Staten says.

The lavender dragon's head nears mine, saliva dripping into my face.

I don't close my eyes. Instead, I growl at my attacker. I'm not a coward. I'm a freaking Pride Leader. The only female dragon since the beginning. I don't need saving. I can do this on my own. With renewed energy and gusto, I launch my attack. My body moves, trying to buck him off of me. My tail swings as my legs kick. Fire erupts from my mouth, and I send it toward the dragon in front of me.

Everyone lands around me, shaking the ground.

Teeth break through my scales. Liquid runs down my neck. My vision is fuzzy. None of this stops my fighting. I can feel my body growing weaker by the moment. No amount of magic will save me. Or will it?

The familiar flame ignites. I let it fill me, let it overtake me. And when I can't contain it any longer, let it blast out from me.

Pressure from my chest lessens. Then the purple dragon is off me. I turn my head and see blurry forms around me. They're going to kill my boys, and I don't have the energy to stop them. My magic is waning. My scales are turning back to human skin. My snout is pressing back into my face. Black hair hides my view of them.

From the sandalwood smell to my right, and the lavender and lemongrass to my left, I know my boys surround me, watching me pass to wherever dragons go. I wish again Bronx could be with me.

I'll miss them all.

"Babe?"

Boroughs, I can still hear them. This dying must take forever.

"Brooklyn?" Manny's sweet voice. My first boyfriend.

"Get up." Staten's harsh voice. Of course, he can't be nice to me even when I'm on my deathbed. "You're not dying. It's only a scratch."

I flip my hair out of my eyes and see eight pairs of eyes staring at me. A collective gasp is released. I lift my arm to see for myself that I'm still whole. I'm glad to see that I'm fully clothed in my badass warrior outfit.

Manny kneels next to me and extends his hand out. I take it, and he guides me to a sitting position. He's such a gentleman.

Everyone takes a step back.

"What happened?" I ask. "How am I not dead?" I look at the five new guys who are hovering. Then my fingers graze my neck.

"I can explain that." A red-haired guy steps forward. "I went in for the killing blow, but your body was turning back into its human form. Something caught my eye, and I stayed my claws. Something told me not to kill you when I saw the jewelry you wear. They glowed and pulsed with something I've never seen before. A blue square line connected them. I immediately turned human so your protectors wouldn't kill us. Shortly after, everyone changed, and we've been waiting for you."

"Can you stand?" Manny asks.

I nod, and he helps me up.

"Hello, I'm Declan. May I see your jewelry?"

I look at Staten. He bows his head ever so slightly. I step forward, toss my hair back, and tilt my head up. Declan traces a finger around my ear, down my neck, and arm, landing on the ring and bracelet on my right hand. My boys growl. He shrugs but then lifts the silver wings with his fingers. "Yeah, you're going to want to come with us," he says.

Chapter Thirty

Declan and his group escort us across the park and toward the Farmleigh House. We walk on a dirt road leading up to a three-story mansion. It's beautiful. I can't wait to see it in the daylight. White and yellow daffodils dot the lawn. A pillared awning covers the main door.

We don't enter through the double wooden doors but rather use a hidden side door in the back. The entire house is dark as we descend into the basement. After two long flights of stairs, we stop before two massive white doors.

"I haven't announced your arrival," Declan says. "Pride Leader Sean might not be here, but we'll get to that." He pushes the solid panels and motions us through.

Is he leading us into a trap? Do I trust him? The enormous room is lit with dozens of sconces hanging from the ceiling. All the walls are white marble, with honey-colored flooring, and dark furniture accented by dark green fabrics.

It has a very old world feeling. I love it.

If this room was on the main floor and it was a castle, the throne would be in the room as royalty oversees a glamorous ball or wedding. A nice seating area is arranged in the far corner.

"I'll go see if I can find Sean," Declan says. "Please stay here. The guys will make sure that you don't wander off."

We watch as Declan exits through an archway. This has been a turn of events that no one expected. We found the dragons, I'm about to meet with Pride Leader Sean, and then we can hurry home and find Bronx.

"Hey, Bronx, we're still in Ireland and now about to meet with their leader. Looks like tomorrow we'll head home and start looking for you. Hang in there."

I don't expect a response, but I'm also reminded that I should check in with Noelle when I get a chance to see what she's found out about the drones.

"Staten?" I opt to communicate with my boys mentally until we know we can trust the Irish Pride.

"Yes?"

"When we get some down time, you should check in with your dad to see if there is anything new?"

He nods.

The wait is killing me. My leg bounces, and then I'm up pacing the room. I feel the eyes of everyone watching me. The Irish guys because they're curious about me being the only female dragon. And my boys, well, they always watch me.

Then the large door that Declan went through opens and in steps an extremely tall man. He has jet-black hair, broad shoulders, and eyes that narrow in on me.

It's late in the evening and not a hair is out of place on him. This, I assume, is Sean. He's wearing dark gray business pants and a crisp, white shirt that's rolled at the sleeves. To say he's intimidating doesn't even cover it. He radiates anger. His head is held high as his shoulders press back. Only his eyes flicker to me and then to my protectors.

Sean's Pride loosely gathers around him. Mine does the same to me. I wait for him to address me.

"Sit," Declan says to us.

We do as we're instructed. Staten to my right and McQueen to my left. Manny keeps watch behind us on the couch. "Hello. I'm Brooklyn Bryer from New York." Sean nods. "I'm sure that Declan has told you what happened earlier?" He nods again. "Good. I'm here on behalf of the New York Pride. I need training, and Mr. Queen suggested your name. As a prominent and respected Leader in the dragon community—"

I've heard my dad spew words to dignitaries and diplomats to placate them. I thought it was appropriate for this situation as well.

Sean holds up a hand. "You can stop with the ass

kissing. I know very well that Queen did not send you to me. I was probably your last choice since none of the others would be willing to degrade themselves to teach another Pride's dragon to become its leader."

"Actually, Mr. ... I didn't get your last name. Declan didn't provide it to me."

"O'Dell."

"Mr. O'Dell, you are my first choice. I've heard great stories about you and how you run your Pride."

"Oh, really? Do tell me some of these stories."

I blanch. He's calling my bluff.

"Pride Leader O'Dell," Staten says. "You are one of the youngest leaders on the oldest Council in Europe. You transitioned about nineteen years ago, when you were twenty-one years old." Oh my, that would make him only forty, my parents' ages. "You have tight control over your members," Staten continues. "But they respect you since you give them a vote in all major decisions. Brooklyn thought you'd be the best to learn from."

"Are you really a dragon?" Sean asks.

"Yes, I am. Didn't Declan and the others tell you?"

"They did, but I need to know for myself."

"Would you like me to show you?" I stand. He stands, too, and nods.

"Clear the room." It doesn't take a second command; his dragons leave us. They don't turn back. "Did you not understand?" he asks.

Oh, he means my Pride, too. I look at my boys and from their faces, they don't want me in a room alone with Sean. Manny and McQueen both have their arms crossed. I don't want to be by myself either, but we need him to teach me. I'll give him anything, almost anything, to get that done, so we can go home and find Bronx.

"It's okay, guys," I tell them. *"I'll holler if I need you, so you better come running."*

"Always," they say as one.

Staten is the last to leave. He turns on his heels and follows his brother out of the same door we entered. When the click of the door sounds, I step behind the couch. My bright green flames encase my body as I peel off my jacket.

"Your dragons can't question you," Sean says. "Ever. You give them a command, and it should be followed." He comes to stand near me but far enough away he won't get hurt during the transformation. "That was your first free lesson."

In a matter of seconds, I'm in my dragon form. The room is so large, I easily fit. By the time I'm searching for Sean, he's in his dragon form, too. He's big, a bit larger than me. And he's beautiful: snow-white. Not like my gorgeous boys, but powerful. It's all encompassing. His scales shine like iridescent pearls. He stalks toward me, but I don't cower. We're both leaders.

In this form, his black eyes are so expressive. We aren't mentally communicating, but I think I know what he wants me to do.

I step forward, closing the distance between us. I hold my head as high as it will go. We're nose to nose. I'm holding my breath, not sure what his next move will be.

His nostrils flare and then his eyes close as he inhales. It's not sexual and vastly different from when my boys smell me in this form. He lets my scent wrap around him, and then his stare penetrates into me. I do the same to him. He smells of warm caramel, sweet, so opposite of his demeanor.

"Mr. O'Dell?" I whisper.

He continues to look at me, my wings, my body. Normally, it'd be weird having a forty-year-old dude checking me out, but this is different. He's not sizing me up for anything. He's genuinely curious about me. I've only ever seen one other Pride Leader: Regan. The night he passed away. We circle each other, letting our tails drag on the floor.

"Brooklyn?"

"Yes!"

His large eye scans my body. My wings twitch from his scrutiny. Now he's giving me the creep factor. Then his voice in back in my mind. *"I will train you, but on one condition, regarding my son and you."*

Chapter Thirty-One

"Excuse me?" I'm back in my human body and barely sitting on the couch. Because of my raised voice, the double doors crash open, and my boys are running toward me. "Whatever it is, absolutely not!"

They stumble to a halt when they see I'm not in any danger. I may not be, but Sean is. My fists clench at my sides and yet my magic thrums throughout my body, on the ready to strike him.

"What's going on?" Staten says. He comes to my side and pulls me back deeper into the couch, trying to defuse the situation. Manny takes my hand and sits on the other open seat, leaving McQueen to glare at Sean. "Again, I ask, what are you yelling about?"

"He'll train me, but he wants something in return that involves his son and me." I point to the Irish Leader. Staten's face whitens. Yeah, that's what I immediately thought, too. And I was just thinking that it's not icky that a forty-year-old was looking at me.

"It's not what you guys are thinking. I don't want her to marry me," Sean says. "But I want an alliance with the New York Pride, and to do that, she must take Declan as her second. He is my son, and it'd be a good match."

It doesn't take long for my protectors to pick up on the key word: match.

"No way!" Manny stands. "Absolutely not."

"It's not done that way in New York," Staten says.

"She's the PL; she can do what she wants," Sean says.

"That may be," I say. "But I'm not marrying your son. I'll offer him the position as my second, but that's all."

"Then we don't have a deal." He gracefully stands and turns.

Boroughs, I can't let him walk away. What about my boys? I won't give them up. I won't share them. I won't bring someone into our circle. I love them. When I marry, it'll be for love. Not obligation. Maybe Declan doesn't even want to marry me.

"It's not a yes," I say to Sean's retreating back. "But I want to discuss this with your Declan."

"What did you just agree to?" McQueen asks. *"Because I thought you said that you'd talk it over with Declan first."*

At least he has the courtesy to have this convo in our minds. *"Look, it's my decision, and I need to learn this. No one else can train me."*

"We can find another PL," Staten says.

"In this short amount of time? We need to leave no later than tomorrow night, so we can find Bronx."

"I know why you are doing this," Manny says. *"But I agree with my brothers. We can find another way."*

The conversation halts when Declan walks through the door. He either knows what his father has done, or he hides it well enough. His face is calm, giving nothing away. "I'm to show you to the guest wing."

My Pride follows him as I grab my duster jacket. I take one more look around the room—a room that has changed my life. I scurry to catch up with the guys. We are led down a hall that's trimmed in dark wood paneling. Golden picture frames hang on the wall showing landscapes, portraits, and animals.

Declan stops before a door. "This is for the guys." He spins and across the hall is another room. "Brooklyn, you can stay here." No one makes a move to enter either room. I know my protectors will stay with me, but I do need a moment with the PL's son. Alone.

"Declan? Could I have a word with you?" I lean my head around him to address the boys. "I'll be okay and will come get you when we're done."

They nod and open the door to their assigned room.

Declan ushers me inside my bedroom but does not close the door. He leaves that choice to me. Instead, he goes and stands next to the balcony and opens the sliding doors.

I lean against the railing, looking out over the property. It has to be well after midnight. It's quiet, and even the bugs are asleep. Something I should be. "I assume that you know the conditions?" I ask. He nods. "While I will do almost anything for my Pride, I can't—won't—marry you."

"I know." He keeps his gaze outward. "It's rare that dragons find that bond. Even more so with a female since you're the first in modern times. I see the way you look at them and how they look at you, even got to witness them protecting you from us. I know what my father wants us to become, but losing them will break you. I see the fire in your eyes, the burn in your heart, and I want that for me someday. Would you be able to give that to me?" He shrugs. "Maybe, but I doubt it. Isn't there a fourth?"

"Yes, but we think the Slayers have him and are holding him hostage to get me to come out of hiding."

He turns to face me. "They know about you?"

"Yeah. I outed myself in hopes to negotiate with the Slayers Council to grant the dragons land. While I didn't turn full on dragon, I changed my skin. I showed my parents, too, and they support me. Us."

"The Bryers of New York. Powerful couple, your folks. And the Council kidnapped your fourth?"

"Right before we came here. Bronx was supposed to meet us at the Eye but never showed."

"This world is going to a shitty mess. How the hell did we get roped into all of this? If you refuse both conditions, he'll know." I know he means his father. "So we'll have to get him to agree to you publicly naming me as your second, agreeing to marry me, but only after you get your fourth back. We'll only marry after we stop the Slayers and after a certain amount of time. I don't know about you, but I'm only twenty years old. I'd like to experience life. Love. Living."

"We could call off the engagement later." He nods. "Say when we're twenty-five."

"No matter what happens, we can't actually marry. Divorce isn't an option. Marriage to a dragon is for life. A unique bond happens. The only way to break it is by death."

"I already have a life bond with Bronx, so how would the marriage bond work?"

He shrugs. "Not sure. It doesn't happen often outside of marriage." He takes my hand. It's warm and nice but different than what I'm used to. "Are you bonded to the others, too?"

I shake my head as I look at our entwined fingers. "Well, I do have a magic bond with Staten."

"That's okay. We can deal with that."

"So, you really are okay with not marrying me and going along with a lie?"

"Yeah."

I gently pull my hands out of his. "Why?"

"Do you want to marry me?" He leans against the banister.

"Like today? No. But I want to be married someday."

"How would that work with your four guys?"

I'll stay single and live with them in the same place. We can have a room for ourselves so I can have space to still call my own.

"Look," Declan says. "I don't know you. We just met today. This isn't old Ireland, and we don't have arranged marriages anymore. The choice should be mine. Yours. Ours. And if we're not meant to be, I don't want to force you or trap you in a loveless marriage. I know that you'll never love me the same way you do your protectors. I don't want to be someone's backup plan any more than you do."

And that's how I know Declan will be an awesome and loving husband to some lucky girl, but that girl won't be me.

Chapter Thirty-Two

Declan leaves after that speech. I scamper across the hall and knock on the door. It immediately opens. Staten is pacing the room. I've never seen him out of sorts before. He's usually calm. Manny sits on the bed, holding his head. He looks shaken. And McQueen still radiates anger with his crossed arms and frown. I sidestep him to get farther into the room. He kicks the door closed.

No one says anything, but they stare at me and watch as I sit next to Manny. Staten leans against the wall, finally stopping his pacing. McQueen opts to take the same stance, just closer to us.

"Declan doesn't want to marry me either, but he will go along with the sham to please his father." I don't look at any of them. "I will name him as my second. We'll find Bronx and figure out what the Slayers are doing. Then we'll announce the engagement between our Prides but won't specify a date. That is the arrangement I have with Declan. If Sean doesn't accept it, then we find another PL *after* we get Bronx back. We'll muddle through me being the leader. If that means we call a gathering of the Pride, so be it."

I meet everyone's gaze. My magic opens, so I can know how they feel about what I just told them. I need them to be okay with it.

Their magic bursts in flares, which I can only assume means they're angry and trying to rein in their emotions.

Staten is the first to break. "If that's what you want, I'll support your decision." He nods at me.

"I don't like it one bit, but I think you know that's what we'd all say," Manny says. "It's a compromise without losing yourself. It's the best you can offer, and I need to be okay with that."

McQueen huffs. "I'll never be okay with watching you and Declan, whatever your relationship will be. I'd prefer it to be one of us to be your second, but it's what's needed for now. You're the PL, so I will support you. But if he ever hurts you, I hope you know that we will kill him. Your second or not."

"I know you all will. But I can handle Declan, his father and whatever blowback I get from this," I say. "I'm making this decision as PL. You don't have to like it. Heck, I don't really like it. But it's what will happen because we need Sean. Just don't tell Bronx yet. I think it needs to come from me. Besides, he needs to focus on himself, not on this." I yawn. "Let's get some sleep. Tomorrow will be a long day of training for me, and we're flying home."

When I wake in the morning, two different arms drape across my belly—my protectors, even in my sleep. Manny's on my right, and McQueen is on my left. I don't need to open my eyes to know that. But Staten's presence isn't felt. That's what causes me to rise.

He's awake, sitting in a chair just outside the patio door. He turns to look at me, smiling.

Carefully, I wiggle my way out from under the blankets and limbs. Yanking my shirt down to cover myself, I pad over to him. "Good morning," I whisper.

He holds out his hand. I take it and sit on his lap. Of the four boys, he's the most cautious with giving me his whole heart. We've been together only that one time, but I still feel close to him. I think he's the most like me, or perhaps it's because he understands me the best.

"How did you sleep?" he asks.

"Like the dead. No visions, no normal dreams. Just sleep."

"You're welcome."

I shift to look into his hazel eyes. "You did that?"

He shrugs. "I figured you needed a peaceful rest."

"You'll need to teach me that."

"I don't think there is much that I really need to teach

you at all. You know it already." He pokes my chest. "It's all in here. You are the one putting limitations on it. You don't think you can do it, or you're not believing it can be done."

I kiss him on the cheek, not wanting to share my morning breath. "I'm sure there's plenty of things I still need to learn from you." I lean my head into the crook of his neck. We sit there and watch the sunrise. "What do you really think of Sean and his son?" I ask.

"Sean is a well-respected leader. While he might seem harsh, we don't hear too much grumbling from his Pride members. Not that they would in front of anyone, but I think we'd know if he treats them poorly."

"Are there some who do?"

He nods. "You'll figure them out. We don't have many dealings with those Prides. PLs can rule how they want. There have been a couple of times where other PLs have stepped in to address items, but for the most part, we leave each other to do our own thing." Staten kisses my forehead. "As for Declan, I knew who he was the minute he changed into his human form. He's the spitting image of his dad, except for the hair color. And I knew him to be around our age."

"What do you know of him?" I lift my head. The snores we hear coming from McQueen make me giggle.

Staten chuckles, too. "I know what you're asking. From

what you've told us, he seems to be a good guy. It shows a lot of his character. I think if you did end up marrying him, he'd do well by you."

"Doesn't matter in the end because I refuse to marry him. I'm eighteen years old; I don't need to marry any one right now. Let alone a stranger. Plus, I kinda thought it'd be one of you guys who I marry. Declan guessed that we're more to each other and pointed out that I couldn't be married to only one of you then. Since Bronx and I are life bonded, Declan didn't know how the marriage bond would work."

"The marriage bond trumps the life bond. It wouldn't null it completely. The terms of both still hold. Bronx's life is tied to yours. The marriage bond goes deeper than that. You'll share a life force, too, but more. It's hard to explain."

"But marriage bonds can be broken? By death?" I think of his birth mom who died, and his dad remarried McQueen's mom.

He shakes his head. "Mom was never bonded to Dad, only in the human sense was she married to him."

"I'm sorry."

"It's fine. There are many days when I miss her. But I have you now in my life. Not that I think of you as my mother, but it's nice having a female who cares about me in my life. I didn't think I'd ever have it after she died. My stepmom, Eliza, is great and all, but it's not the same."

"Staten." I turn his head to face mine. "Not only do I care about you, but I love you. You and your brothers mean the world to me. Everything I am is because of you. I'd give you anything you ask of me. I gave you my heart a long time ago. I thought you knew that."

"I do know. But it's nice to finally hear you say it." He leans in and kisses me.

Morning breath, be damned. We've been sitting here for the past fifteen minutes, and he hasn't told me to brush my teeth. I kiss him back with everything I have, pouring my heart into the kiss. His arms snake around my waist, pulling me closer. He deepens the kiss with a brush of his tongue. I open and let him in. My fingers run through his silky hair. All thoughts of marriages and my new second in command vanish.

It's just this. Us, out here.

He lifts me to straddle him in the chair as his hands roam under my shirt. I tug his off completely, needing to feel his smooth skin. His lips trail kisses down my neck. A small moan escapes me. Staten's fingers grip my thighs.

I can feel his magic humming beneath his skin. He's losing control. It's coaxing mine out, too. I try to smash that down. We can't lose ourselves. His brothers are just in the next room. Neither of us comment about it, nor at this moment do we care.

Bright green magic rushes out of me.

Staten breaks contact, then sees the light and smiles.

I'm hot. My body is heating up, and it's not from the heavy make-out session. Well, part of it probably is. This is something more, though. Staten turns my hand over and drops his eyes to my palm. I follow his gaze.

There, hovering is a green and white flame, swirling around and pulsing. I've never seen anything like it before. "What is it?" I ask.

"It's part of your soul."

Did I just call part of me to bond with Staten? Is that how Bronx did it? Without further questions or hesitation, I cup the flame and lower my hand to Staten's bare chest. I force the flame into him. He shoots forward, wrapping his arms around me so I don't fall from his lap.

"You didn't have to life bond with me," he says. "We already have the magic bond."

"I guess I should have asked you first."

"I would have said yes. Anything in my power is yours. I will protect you until our deaths."

Oh, man. This just got heavy. I don't regret bonding with him, but it weighs on my heart knowing that now his life force is locked with mine. I don't need to ask the question floating in my mind. After I thought it, I answered it myself. Since we're bonded, if one of us dies, we all die.

Chapter Thirty-Three

We head inside. Manny and McQueen are up. Both grin at us like they know we've been kissing. Their eyes drop to our linked hands.

"Morning," I say.

"Yes it is, Babe." He winks.

Manny nods.

"We were about to wake you to see if we can find Sean, so we can get today started." I straighten my shirt with my free hand.

A knock on the door silences us from divulging any more details. Manny goes and opens the door.

Declan stands there. "Hello," he says. "Did everyone sleep okay?" His eyes lock onto my hand holding Staten's and then to everyone's bare chests. He doesn't comment. "I'm here to escort you to breakfast. And then after, Brooklyn, you can go meet with my dad."

We make Declan wait while we change clothes, then follow him back down the hall and up a flight of stairs into a massive kitchen. It's by far the largest I've ever seen. It doesn't blend with the old world feeling of the rest of the house. The black stainless-steel appliances and black marbled countertops are a stark contrast to the cream walls and honey-colored flooring.

A dozen other people are seated around the dining table. On it are platters and bowls filled with various foods from eggs to meats to waffles. The aroma of coffee and bacon immediately grab my attention.

A hush descends on the room as my party enters. All eyes follow my movements around the kitchen. I notice right away I'm the only female in the room. My safety is not a concern, though. Declan is in front of me, Staten still holds my hand, McQueen is on my other side, and Manny follows behind.

The PL's son pulls out a chair near the head of the table and motions for me to sit. He sits next to the head position. My boys take open seats to my right. Eventually, quiet chatting resumes as Declan passes me dishes. My Pride eats in silence, observing the others.

I'm about take a bite of breakfast when the Irish dragons stand as one. A door opens and in walks Sean. He gestures for everyone to sit. He does have them trained well. They each bow their heads toward their leader, a sign of respect or a non-verbal good morning.

Declan slides his hand under the table and pats my knee.

The movement startles me and I jerk. My Pride glares at Declan, their expressions softening when they confirm that I'm okay.

"What happened?" Staten asks.

"It's nothing," I say to him, turning my attention to Sean. "Declan and I would like a moment of your time after breakfast."

The PL nods and continues eating. When he sees that everyone is about finished, he says, "Everyone. Please hold on for a moment. I'd like to introduce our guests." He waves in our direction. "This is Brooklyn Bryer from the New York Pride. She and her ..."

"Protectors," I say.

"She and her protectors have my blessing for the duration of their stay. Please grant them the respect that you show to me and my son."

As one, the Irish dragons bow to us and leave the room.

I open my magic to my boys and ask them to leave the room, too. They comply immediately. Staten is the last to leave and squeezes my hand on his departure. I wonder if he's thinking of our bond. He hasn't left my side since, and normally he doesn't have the need for constant physical contact with me.

"I gather you two have discussed the matter?" Sean asks after the doors click shut.

"We have," I say. "I will accept your son as my second

in command. We can announce that publicly when you want to. But before we tell anyone of our engagement, I need to find a fourth member of my protectors. He was taken before I came here. It's imperative that we find him. We believe that the Slayers have him and are holding him hostage in exchange for something. Probably myself."

"After her protector is found," Declan says, "and *after* she finds out what the Slayers want, there will be an announcement of the engagement."

"We will leave tonight to go back home, find Bronx, figure out the Slayers' next move, and I'll return here. That is the bargain. Do we have a deal?"

"I am hearing rumors of the York Academy using drones to find the dragons," Sean says. "They are equipped with lasers, and when a dragon is found in the sky, it scans and records the body to identify it. They want to know our numbers, identifying markings, etc., all being downloaded someplace to be analyzed."

What the boroughs? How does he know that?

"Some fly during the night hours, while others are launched during the day," he continues. "Their second phase is to equip the drones with titanium tracking or some poison-tipped darts to capture the dragons. They are using magic and embedding it into the technology. The possibilities are endless once they get a handle on exactly how to mold the magic and get it to stick."

If that's true, we need to be really careful. And I need to confirm this with Noelle and Danzel, but it feels correct. How many more of us must die before we can have peace?

"I got them to agree to giving the New York Pride land, and I've expected them to renege on that promise," I say. "My parents are working to find out information and to assist in any way they can."

"Yes, I heard that, too. You showed them your dragon form," Sean says.

I nod; there's no use denying it. Besides, I told Declan that last night anyway.

Sean continues, "Allister is a power-hungry man and will do anything to keep that power. He does want to kill all the dragons, so he can add that title to his resume. He'll go down in history as the one to cull the earth of the beasts."

"He's going down in history all right. If I have anything to do with it, he'll be wiped off the face of the earth. He's allowed too many of us to die. Even when I was a slayer, he was reckless with our lives. No more. It ends. One way or another."

"Spoken like a true leader." Sean stands. "Speaking of, Declan, would you please see to our guests? I believe they left their belongings at a hotel. They'll need to go back and check out. Return here and assist them in making arrangements home." Declan nods and leaves us. "Now,

Brooklyn. Come walk with me."

Sean is dressed again in a pressed gray suit. He stands tall, exuding power even when walking. I'm not short by any means, but I barely come up to his shoulders. He leads us out of the house and onto a walking path.

Now seeing the property in the daylight, it confirms my suspicions. The landscape is breathtaking, green as far as the eye can see. Trees, tall grasses, and wildflowers bloom everywhere. The lawn near the house is kept trimmed. Cars line up near the main door.

"We use this property like the slayers use Columbia University. While the main and upper floors are kept for the tourists, the level below we have remodeled for our own use. There are many months of the year where 'renovations' are being done to certain rooms or floors, so we can have more access when we host Pride gatherings." I assumed it was like that. "There is no secret, really, to being the PL," Sean continues. "It's a matter of believing you are and having direct control over your dragons, which in a sense you do. You're connected to them, correct?"

"Yes. When I finally acknowledged what I am, their voices flooded into my mind. Staten had to show me how to block them out."

"He's the tallest of the three, correct?" I nod. "Yes, I can feel his power. I'd keep him around and close to me if I were you."

"We're magic and life bonded, so that won't be a problem. If I hadn't taken Declan as my second, it probably would have been Staten."

Sean stops walking and gazes down at me. "Excuse me? You're life bonded with him?"

I swallow. "Yes."

"But he's not your mate?"

I shake my head.

"That's very interesting."

I don't mention that I have a life bond with another. "May I ask you something?" It's his turn to nod. "How come you're not surprised that I'm a dragon?"

"Oh, trust me, when I heard the rumors there was finally a female in our midst, I was surprised. I'm curious as to why none of the other Prides reached out to you to strike a bargain of sorts."

"To use me as a weapon?"

"Possibly. But to show the others that they have something that they do not."

"Is that what you're doing?"

"No. I'm looking out for my son. He will not be the PL after I'm gone."

"How do you know that?"

"I've foreseen it. We are a small pride, much smaller than yours. It could be because we've been kept on the island, or that times are changing. Our numbers are dwindling. Some of the dragon couples are no longer having children, for whatever some genetic reason. Sons are not being born but females are. But you are the first to actually be a dragon, so there is hope for us after all. Maybe there is hope for the girls yet. They could be late bloomers."

Now, that is sad. I hadn't expected him to say that to me. He's very open about matters. Maybe for the ones closest to his heart.

"Did you foresee me?"

He shakes his head. "I do know of the dragon with four Protectors, though. That was foretold centuries ago. I just never thought it would be a female." He smiles. "Continuing on with the lessons, to be a great leader, you need to put the Pride first. Listen to them. I don't mean the petty stuff, the real concerns. Let them know that you truly care for them and hear them. They must feel that you would do absolutely anything within your power to help them."

"I would."

"Then show them. Not with words, with actions."

"May I ask you something?"

"Yes, go ahead."

"When Declan saw my jewelry, that's what caused him to stop fighting. He said that power emitted from them. Is that why he decided to allow us to come see you?"

Sean doesn't look at me but instead gazes out over the fields. He takes a long time, as if gathering his thoughts. So long that I don't think he'll answer my question. Finally, he says, "It takes immense power to infuse inanimate objects with magic. You don't even need to tell me that it's Staten's magic in those earrings because I can see it. The necklace, ring and bracelet have a bit of him in there, too, so he must have helped the others. They still pulse with it. It's also why I know you and he are magically bonded." He stops and turns to me. "Have the others given you magic items as well?"

"Why?"

"Not only is powerful magic used to do it, but the recipient of the items also must wield enough to invoke the magic that was infused with the object. You did so when it blasted out. Declan said it was nothing like he's ever seen. It feels like a stun but more forceful. Depending on what was used, the outcome of protection could be different. It's very old magic, and not a lot of people know about it. But apparently your protectors do, and you are strong enough to use it. Another rarity. So I don't think I really need to teach you it. It's already inside of you. You just have to unlock it, hone it, and use it."

Sean and I walk around the grounds for a few more hours. He tells me things I already know or at least can guess. He runs his Pride like a company. He's president,

CEO, and CFO. The second does all the technology related items, so I guess I'd call him the CTO. And even though Declan isn't his second, he has shown great interest in the technology area. Apparently, he's got a knack for it.

He advises to keep my protectors around me at all times and keep the current Council intact so that the Pride has stability. Like I'd send my boys away. Two of them are literally a part of me now. Make small changes at first. Get them to see the benefits before doing anything drastic.

Well, I can do that. I'll show them and talk with them. The whole trip kinda feels like a waste and we could have been rescuing Bronx. But I have learned a lot and sometimes it was things I needed to hear from a third party. Sean said the secret of being a leader is that there is no secret. Rule with a good heart, and the rest will fall into place.

First order of business will be to call a meeting after Bronx is safe.

Chapter Thirty-four

By the time Sean and I are back in the house, my boys have returned from checking out of the hotel. I find them in Declan's room booking us a flight home. Leaning against the door jam, I listen to their conversation. I need them to get along since we'll be bringing Declan into our tight knit group.

"As far as we know, we weren't followed here, so we can take a direct flight back," Staten says.

"Okay, but just in case," Declan says, "I'll pay for it, and you can just transfer funds into our accounts." Staten nods and swipes his phone to move money around. "I assume that you'll all want seats close to each other?" Manny nods. "Okay. Shouldn't be a problem." He continues keying in information and after a few more minutes, he says, "We're all booked. The flight is leaving in three hours from now. I need to get packed, and then we should head out."

"We?" I ask.

"I'm going with you. I'm your second now." Declan's

head tilts to the side. "My father will make a formal announcement. He's called all of us back to the dining room in twenty minutes."

"Okay, I'll go shower and change and meet everyone there." I turn to my guys. "Is my luggage in the bedroom?"

"Yes," Manny says. "I'll come with you."

"Thank you."

We leave Declan's room and find our way back to ours. Manny pushes the door open for me.

"You life bonded with Staten this morning." It's a statement. "McQueen and I felt it." He hangs his head.

"I'm sorry." I hadn't realized that they would feel it. Knowing them, they'd want to have the bond with me, too. "Why didn't you say something after Bronx? If you already knew when that happened. I didn't think … I know you would bond with me if I asked you. We just haven't had the chance to. An opportunity presented itself when Staten and I were alone." I press my finger to his chin, forcing him to look at me. "I understand what it means to you, Manny. And I'm asking you this now—not as a second choice or third, but because I truly want you to. I am asking you to life bond with me."

"Of course, I will." He smiles. "And not because I asked about it, forcing you to ask me. I know you'd ask me at some point. But I want this now. Life is too short to wait. It's time I went after what I want. And that's you." His magic instantly appears in his palm, white mixing with his dark green. He presses it into my chest as I jerk back. His strong hand grips my shoulder to steady me.

I feel his magic floating around inside my body, and then it settles near my heart. The slivers of Bronx and Staten greet Manny's and lock together like another puzzle piece clicking into place, my soul relaxes into a peaceful and steady rhythm.

Manny drops to a knee. "Thank you. I am your servant. Anything you desire is yours if it's in my power. I'll protect you until my last breath."

I sink to his level and kiss him, so he knows how much he means to me. We're both kneeling and wrapped in each other's arms. Before things can get carried away, I pull back. "I love you, Manny." I lightly kiss his lips again. "But I need to shower and change, so we can get to the meeting and leave."

"I know. Bronx is on my mind, too. We'll find him."

He stands and helps me up, ushering me into the bathroom where I quickly change and shower. By the time the water stops, there is a knock on the door.

"You about ready, Brooklyn?" Manny asks.

"Yep, I'll be right out." I quickly run my fingers through my hair, throw on jeans and a clean T-shirt. "Let's go."

We are the last to arrive to the dining room. Sean waves me to his side. Declan is already there. I suck in a breath as Manny walks me to the front. He stops where his brothers stand, so I continue the few remaining steps by myself.

"Thank you for coming so quickly," Sean says. "Sit." Everyone does. "I have some great news to share. Our guests from New York are leaving shortly, but Ms. Bryer has agreed to certain conditions." He turns his head to me.

"Thank you, Sean, for your hospitality." I nod, addressing the room. "I am the leader of the New York Pride, and I name Declan O'Dell as my second in command. He'll be leaving with us." Chatter rises throughout the room about my naming one of their own as my second. But I think it's more about me being a female dragon. Sean quiets them with a clearing of his throat. "There are some other things going on at York Academy that must be addressed before further announcements are made. But rest assured that I, my protectors and Pride, will treat my new second with respect. I will lead by example and vow that no harm will come to him by my own hand or claw."

"I know we sprung this on most of you," Sean says. "If you'd like to say goodbye or wish Declan well, do so quickly as he'll be leaving shortly."

The room bursts in voices. A line forms on the side of the room where Declan is standing. Many want to express their well wishes. A couple of guys hug him and tell him to call often.

A few strangers come to shake my hand and offer us goodbyes as well. Seeing the Irish Pride behaving like a loving family, this is what I want for New York. I want us to quit the squabbling and inner attacks and be there for each other. They need to listen and stop doing stupid things that will for sure get themselves killed. I guess I do have my work cut out for me.

Eventually, Declan is ready to go. He gives his dad a hug. "Remember what we discussed," Sean whispers in his ear.

Declan nods and steps away. He turns and smiles at me, holding his hand out. My eyes drop to his waiting palm. Slowly, I take it. He lifts it up and squeezes my fingers. Shouts of praise rise throughout the room.

We walk through the house and out the front door. A large SUV waits to take us to the airport.

"What do you think that comment was about?" Staten asks me.

"I don't know, but I will find out."

The flight back to New York City is long. Declan and I sit together, while all three of my boys sit across from us. Needless to say, none of them are happy about it, and Declan refuses to switch seats with any of them. I tell them to let it be. They can listen in and watch me from across the aisle.

"Bronx?" I say. *"We're on our way home. If you can hear me, be ready. We're coming for you."*

I don't get a reply, but I hadn't expected to. He'll be waiting for us. I quickly send off a text to Noelle, too, letting her know we're on our way back. Of course, it's coded so I hope she can figure it out.

"Get some sleep, Brooklyn," Declan says. "We have six hours to go, and it'll be the early morning when we land."

"What did your dad mean about remembering what you guys talked about?"

"He's reminding me to live up to the expectations of being your second. He still thinks we're going to marry at the end of this, and I'm to ensure that it happens. He said that it'd be easier if we fell in love and then marriage would be the obvious next step, but also that I'm to help you with figuring out the Academy's plans. In the long run, whatever they have planned might affect the rest of the Prides. All eyes are on us now. We've got to make it count."

It doesn't go unnoticed that he's said "we" and "us" in his speech. "But, remember, that we're not a 'we' or 'us'. You are my second and will not be anything more to me than a friend. I won't marry you." He seems to be a genuinely nice guy. Maybe I'm just waiting for the other shoe to drop. The trip to Ireland and finding a PL to train me was just too easy. But everything that Sean said was obvious. There is no key or trick to being a good leader.

My eyes are heavy, and I do need sleep. I hope that Bronx is resting, too, so I can see him again. I'm rewarded when I open my dream eyes and see him standing in his dark green dragon form.

"Hello, Sweetheart." Bronx lifts his head and watches me land onto the ground next to him. *"I've been waiting for you. I got your message that you're on your way back. I'm sorry I didn't respond. You don't want to know what they were doing, but I do have some news to share."*

"I miss you, Bronx." I nuzzle his neck. *"And I have a feeling I know exactly what they are doing to you. I've been feeling phantom pains, and I think they're coming from you."*

"I'm sorry I can't control some of it. It's seeps out before I can stop it." He returns my affection. *"While they were ... never mind. I heard someone talking about the weapons facility. They are stock piling and creating something new."*

"Besides the dart drones?"

"Yes. But how did you know about those?"

"Sean, the Irish PL, told me about it."

"Hmm. Okay. Allister is pulling every favor owed to him because production has been kicked into high gear. Prototypes are being made and tested out in the real world."

"What else besides the drones is he creating?"

"Remember those titanium arrows that McQueen was shot down by? Something like those, but better."

How could that even be possible?

"Do you know where the weapons facility is?" I ask.

"No, they didn't say."

"Maybe we can get Noelle to find out, if she doesn't already know."

"We're going to need to take that place offline. Cripple them to even the playing field."

I lift my head to gaze into his eyes. *"What aren't you telling me?"*

"Nothing for you to worry about."

"I still will, though."

"I know. Oh, hey, I felt you bond with Staten and Manny. That must have been a shock for Manny that you and I were bonded before him. Was he mad?"

"No. Disappointed. But it's all good between us."

"So that leaves McQueen."

"I guess it does."

He's the only one I haven't said I love you to, nor have we had sex. While I'm sure he would want to, there hasn't been an opportunity, nor has it been on my mind. We've got other things to worry about than my love life.

McQueen is also the newest member of my protectors. Even though I've lived with his family for a couple of days, I hardly know him. If Manny could feel when I bonded with Bronx and Staten, then McQueen must've felt it, too. I should at least discuss it with him and learn his thoughts on the matter. Maybe he doesn't even want to be bonded to me like his brothers.

Chapter Thirty-five

We land at Kennedy Airport and have two vehicles waiting for us. Since it's nearly three in the morning, Danzel didn't think Allister would be watching us. Plus, Declan bought the tickets. Staten and McQueen instruct each driver to take the long way through the city. I'm in the vehicle sandwiched between McQueen and Declan. McQueen casually lays his arm around my shoulder, clearly a possessive gesture. I lean into him, giving my own sign to Declan.

I check my phone for any messages from Noelle. It's too early in the day, and she should be sleeping. She better respond by tomorrow. We need answers. Now.

It takes us an hour to navigate around the city, making sure that no one is following us. We do spot a couple of drones out, so we're extra cautious, sitting low in the backseats. I took a nap during most of the flight; now, I'm wide awake. By the time we arrive at McQueen's house, I feel like exercising. I haven't had a good workout in days, and my body is feeling it.

"Hey before everyone goes their separate way, I need to tell you guys something," I say. "I'm not sure how to say this ... so I'm just going to. They're torturing Bronx. I spoke with him during the plane ride over the pond. He doesn't know for sure who took him, but he thinks Allister is behind it. Those phantom pains I was having, it's from him, because of our bond. So get some rest and later this morning, we're hitting it hard and finding him. He's priority number one."

"We should scout tonight," Manny says.

"No. We need rest. We've been traveling for a couple of days and we don't know what we'll run into when we find him. All of us need to be well-rested and keep our wits. I won't have you guys going after him without thinking things through." Staten smiles, showing me his dimples. *"What?"* I ask through our mental connection.

"You're becoming a true leader. Taking charge, giving us orders. It's nice seeing a different side of you. It means you're growing as a person."

"I agree with Brooklyn's assessment of the situation," Declan says. "I know you guys don't know me well. But you trust her. I trust her. And she's right. We don't know enough to go barreling into anything half-cocked. We'll only get ourselves hurt or dead." He looks at each of them. "And I know you don't want the latter."

McQueen nods and then shows Declan a room that is on

the opposite side of the house from where our rooms are. Declan doesn't say anything about it. And really, what's to stop him from walking the length of the hallway to get to me? He bids us goodnight and closes the door.

Manny and Staten opt to go to bed since they watched over me while I slept next to Declan. I'm alone in the gym, already done with stretching and about ready to step onto the treadmill.

"Up for some company, Babe?" McQueen leans against the doorway.

"Always." I motion for him to join me. "I feel like we haven't worked out in ages. I slept for most of the flight, so I might as well do something productive."

"It has been a while." McQueen stretches.

I start the machine and walk at a steady pace, waiting for McQueen to finish and match my strides. He jumps on and we're off. The steady beat of our feet slapping the black track soothes me. McQueen keeps glancing my way. I know he wants to tell or ask me something but doesn't.

I'm guessing it's about the bond.

I don't comment on it. If he wants to bring it up, then he has to break the ice. It's weird that he hasn't said anything yet, especially since he's supposed to be brazen about things. But this trip has him off kilter. He's been quiet and reserved. Plus, we haven't had any real alone time until now. But now we're back at his parents' house doing exactly what we did before the mission. I wonder if things will change between us.

The hour goes by, and we finally stop running. We decide to do some strength conditioning. I think he's pushing himself, and that's pushing me harder. He spots me for a while, and then I do the same for him. After we're both exhausted from lifting weights, we take a much-needed water break.

It's during this down time that I think McQueen is going to ask me about the bond. He doesn't. Instead, he asks about my time with Sean. "What did he say to you?" he asks.

"Nothing I didn't already know."

It does make me wonder where Sean got all is information. He must have spies at the school or possibly even dragons that are friendly to his Pride. Neither would surprise me.

McQueen calls it quits, telling me that I do need to sleep, even if I'm not tired. By the afternoon, I'll be dragging. I tell him that I'm going back to my room to shower and change and possibly to lie down. He leaves me but lingers at his door as he watches me enter my room. Why hasn't he said anything about the bond? I know he wants to. Perhaps he's waiting for me to ask him. I do want to bond with all of my boys. They need to be part of me. They're already on my mind all the time. They might as well be in my heart, too.

As I get ready, I text Noelle again since it's imperative that we talk or meet today.

Me: Hey, I've been sick lately and need to be rescued from the house. Please kidnap me so we can have fun outside. Mom won't let me go anywhere.

It's still early, and I don't expect a response. My room is dark, and I'm busy looking at the phone screen. The tiny hairs on my arms rise.

A shadow moves near my bed. I flip on the light, and Declan is standing there. My hand slaps over my mouth to stop the scream that's on the tip of my lips. "Boroughs, you scared me." I breathe in a deep breath. "Did you need something?"

"No. I couldn't sleep and didn't know where you were, so I thought I'd wait here for you." Okay, but that's still sort of uber creepy if you ask me. "I don't think your protectors would want me wandering around the house by myself. Then I thought that they probably wouldn't want me waiting in here for you, either. I know they don't trust me."

"I'm sorry, Declan. Someone should have showed you around." I walk closer to the bed now that my heartbeat is under control. "Have you ever been to the States before?"

He shakes his head. "No, I haven't."

"All right. Later today, I'll give you the dime tour. If it's not safe for me to be out, then hopefully, my friend Noelle who is coming to the house can take you after she tells us about the drones, Allister's plans, and anything else she's found out."

"Is she an instructor or on the Council?" He gestures to the bed as if asking permission to sit. I nod.

I busy myself with selecting clothes to change into. "No, she's a student. But since the last battle that took place at the school, the dragons killed so many of them the Council had to scramble to get enough teachers, and I'm told they consolidated classes. Last I heard, Level Threes were taken out of missions and are solely learning about drones."

"I'd be interested in the drones' tech."

"Same here, so I hope Noelle has much to tell us." I hold up my arms with my clothes. "I'm going to take a shower. If you want to wait here you can, then we'll go grab some breakfast."

"Aren't you going to rest?"

"No, maybe I'll take a nap later today."

"All right."

I leave Declan sitting on my bed. Should I feel weird about that? Possibly. A stranger who is my second and who I've known all for forty-eight hours is in my bedroom while my boyfriend—boyfriends—are just down the hall. But there is something comforting about his presence.

After I emerge from the bathroom, Declan and I go in search for food. We are still the only ones awake, and we rummage in the kitchen as quietly as we can. The only thing I know how to make is scrambled eggs, so that's what

I offer.

He helps me crack the shells but keeps getting tiny bits in the mix. I can tell that he's never done it before by the careful way he's working. It's not good. He keeps fishing out the little white flakes. Finally, I hand him a bowl and tell him to measure the flour, which I also hand him, and then the eggs mixture. He should be able to make pancakes.

His whisking is too violent, and batter is tossed in all directions. It lands on the counter, on his face, and on my clothes. We laugh at our antics. I swipe a rather large doughy piece from his cheek. It doesn't come clean off; instead, it makes it worse, which makes me double over in more laughter.

And this is how my protectors see us when they walk into the kitchen.

"What's going on?" McQueen asks.

"Um, sorry about the mess," I say. "We were hungry and wanted to make breakfast for you guys."

"I guess we got a bit carried away," Declan says. "I'll clean it up."

Manny takes a dish towel and starts wiping the counters while McQueen takes out the large skillet and pours the batter into round circles. Staten opens the fridge and removes syrup, then takes out plates from the cabinet.

The kitchen is silent, except for the rattling of cookware. I wish someone would start talking. My boys need to include Declan. He's family now, whether we like it or not.

Maybe that person should be me. "Declan was telling me that he's never been here to New York. So after we hear from Noelle, I thought we'd go take him to see some sights. Of course, we'll be on the lookout for the drones and we'll use the tourist thing as a front to search for Bronx." I take a bite of fluffy eggs. "When I talked with Bronx last night, he said he's doing okay and knows that we're back home and will start looking for him after we touch base with Noelle and Danzel. He doesn't know where he is, and they've drugged him. All he knows is that he's in a basement or underground dwelling. He said it's musty smelling. During his time there, he's managed to figure out something is going on with titanium arrows." I look at McQueen. "You know, the kind they used on you. Bronx thinks they're being mass-produced now."

"That's not good if it's true." He cringes as he massages his chest where the arrow hit him a few weeks ago. "Nasty things. Wouldn't want to wish that hell on anyone."

"Why?" Declan asks. "Was it made differently or something?"

"The entire arrow and shaft were made of titanium. Normally, what we see over here are just the arrows tips made of metal. They alone cause enough damage. But now the shafts are coated or treated with it, and it makes getting hit all the more potent. I'm leaning toward coating since it flaked off, and some particles got stuck under the skin even while the arrow was removed. It weakened my body because we didn't know fragments were still in there. I didn't figure it out until the next day when I couldn't heal all the way. Imagine a shot to a vital organ." He shakes his head. "Not good."

The vibration of my cell phone draws my attention. Everyone else pats their pockets. I pull out mine and look at the screen.

Noelle: YES! I'm coming over right now!! I've called an Uber, and we'll see if we can do a covert op and get you out from under Mom's nose. I have so much to catch you up on!!!
Me: 710 Arrow Moon Sliver, Queens

"Noelle is on her way here," I say. "Not sure what she told the school to leave, but she said that she has lots to tell us."

Yes. Finally, I feel like we're about to move forward instead of this waiting game. There are too many moving parts and not enough information to make any reasonable decisions.

Chapter Thirty-Six

By the time we clean up breakfast and the dishes, the doorbell rings. I sprint down the hallway and into the foyer. McQueen is right behind me, using his long strides to catch up. I yank open the door, and there is my best friend. It's only been a couple of days, but it feels way longer than that.

She looks good. Rested, even. Noelle has light makeup on her face, her hair is styled, and she's smiling. "Hiya, BFF!" She flings her arms around me. "Miss me? I sure missed you." She peers around me. "Your guys, too. School is just not the same without all the drama going on."

"Of course, I missed you like crazy." I turn my head, and all four guys are standing there. "Come on in." I step aside to let her in through the door.

"Oh, we've got plenty to keep us all busy, but nothing like what happened when you guys came into Brooklyn's life," Noelle continues. "Now that is a soap opera where I need front row seats, a bag of popcorn, and the rewind button hot at my fingertips." We continue to the living room, and Noelle is still chatting. "How was wherever you went?" She sinks onto the couch and turns her attention to Declan. "I see you picked up a straggler on the way. Who are you?"

"I'm Declan and Brooklyn's second in command."

Her mouth drops open. "Wait, I thought that one of you guys," she points to my protectors who have opted to sit around us in the chairs, "would be her second. If I were a betting gal, it would have been Staten."

"It was part of a deal I made with his PL," I say.

"PL?"

"Pride Leader. It's nothing for you to worry about. Just know that he'll be hanging around from now on, and anything you say to me, he can be trusted so you can say in front of him, too." Boroughs, I hope I'm not wrong about Declan.

"Um, can I get some water or coffee? I kinda ran out of the school as soon as I could."

"Of course, Noelle." Manny stands.

"Oh, no." She tugs my arm. "We'll get it."

Subtle much? But I let her pull me up from the couch and haul me toward the kitchen.

"Okay, for realz, who is that yummy man? Please do not tell me that he's yours, too. I don't think I can handle that."

"It's not like that, Noelle. He's just my second. He

knows about my boys."

"And he's okay with it?"

"He has to be. I won't give them up, even for him or his father."

"What does his dad have to do with it?"

"His dad wants us to marry."

"What? Get the heck out of here. You're only eighteen."

"I know." I open the fridge and hand her a bottle of water.

She brushes it aside. "Forget about that. I want deets on this arranged marriage."

"We're not having one. My priority is Bronx, finding him, and bringing him home. All this other stuff is secondary to that." I start to walk back into the living room, because we truly do need to formulate a plan on rescuing Bronx.

Noelle grabs my shirt's sleeve. "Can I have him, then?"

"Who? Declan?" She nods. "I know you said that I don't have any magic, and it's only been a few weeks since Sax died, but I've gotta tell you, girl, the moment I saw him … If stars could align themselves, I think they would."

"By all means, then. Who am I to stop the universe from telling Noelle Arden no?"

"Exactly."

"I feel bad for Declan. He's not going to know what hit him."

"Hey, now. Be nice."

"Oh, I am."

I link her arm through mine, and we saunter back to the boys. I'm glad to see that no one has died. In fact, they are talking about tech stuff. My guess is something about the drones. Most of that is way over my head. It's not that I don't find it interesting. I do. I just don't have the knack for mechanics.

"Okay, back to the business at hand," Noelle says. "Since you guys left to go wherever you went, Mr. Astor has been hell bent on revamping the school. All levels are going out on nightly missions. Because there are so few of us, we all go. It's been a free for all since the night that ... you know. Anyway. All Year Threes, instead of attending classes, are doing a special assignment. I have it on good authority that they are the ones flying the drones around the city. At first it was just at night, and now they are out in broad daylight. Some of the students analyze the data as it comes in."

"What are they programed to look for?" Declan asks.

"Dragons. They scan the skies for them and when they find one, they shoot a specialized formula tranq dart to immobilize them. The mission is to capture one or more alive, study the genetics and magical properties, and see if they can be flipped and used by the Slayers as their weapons and if they can't figure it out ..."

Oh, boroughs. That is not what I expected to hear Noelle say. "I'd like to hear any ideas you might have," I say, looking at everyone in the room.

"If it were me," Declan says, "I'd get a small team together, find the facility, and take it out by any means necessary."

"And how would you do that?" Staten asks. "We don't even know where it is."

"I could find that out," Noelle says. "The guy giving me this information might tell me more."

"And what if he's telling Allister or feeding you false information?"

She slumps in her seat. "I didn't think of that."

"Let me go with you when you talk to your guy." Declan stands. "I'll see what he knows and get him to talk."

"Just don't kill him," I say. "We can't have more eyes on us, and I don't want anything to happen to Noelle."

He nods.

I look between him and my best friend. She could be correct about him. There is something about them. I've caught them both gazing at each other. I bring forth a small amount of my magic to see their auras. Both shine and swirl. While Declan's is bright white, Noelle's is still muted by her lack of magic. But they are entwining. I guess only time will tell. My second and BFF. It could work.

Since I'm done being Miss Match Maker, I move onto

the more important topic; Bronx. "How are we going to get Bronx back? Any suggestions?"

"We should use your life bond link and locate him," Staten says. "Then once we know where he is, we can formulate a plan to break him out. Right now, we're flying blind."

"Then what, drive around the city until we find him?"

"No, Brooklyn. You should be able to find him. He's part of you. Just as he knows where you are and what you feel, you should be able to locate him through that. It'll take practice; I can help you now that we're bonded."

I glance a look at Noelle and Declan, but neither pay attention to me or our conversation.

"Then let's get going on that. Noelle." The sound of her name makes her jump and look at me. "I want you and Declan to go back to school and find out more about the weapons facility. Then report back here, so we can devise a plan. Bring Manny with you in case you run into trouble. I'll stay here with Staten and work on my magic." I look at McQueen. "I need you to chat with your dad and let him know what happened in Ireland, who Declan is, and what we've just decided this morning."

"As you wish." He leaves the room.

Everyone else lingers and chats for a bit to figure out who's driving, what time they're leaving, and should return. I just hope that they'll be okay.

Chapter Thirty-Seven

We'll gather again later this evening to get a plan in place on what we're going to do about the facilities and how to rescue Bronx. Staten and I head to the basement after everyone else leaves the house. We pull out the floor mats, resuming our positions across from each other on the ground.

"Brooklyn, open your magic and find the part that is Bronx. Think of him. How he looks, how he makes you feel, the sound of his voice." I nod, letting him know that I've found it. "Now imagine a line connecting that part of him that's inside of you to him, where he is physically."

I do as Staten suggests and imagine a rope tied on one end that's anchored in me and floating out to him. It's loose and waffling, but it's there. I can see it in my mind as clear as my hand in front of me.

"Elongate it and stretch it outward, letting it lead you to him. It should know where to look. Your mind should take you there."

The picture is dark. Everything is black. Slowly, it changes to color, like a TV warming up. His large frame is hunched over a chair he's strapped to. His head hangs low, almost to his chest. Blood drips to the gray cement floor from open gashes on both his forearms. His shirt is grimy with caked bloodstains, sweat, and dirt.

His chest rises and falls.

I look around the room; it's empty except for Bronx.

His head snaps up as if he knows someone is in the room with him. Dull green eyes dart around, searching for something. He tenses and then jerks in the chair.

"Bronx?" I say. "It's me. Can you feel me?"

"Sweetheart?"

"Yes. I'm trying to find you. Relax and tell me where you are."

"I don't know. I've been in this room for a few days now. Since the last time we spoke."

"Hold on because we're coming for you. Soon."

I can't look at his broken and beaten body. My fists clench at my sides. Anger bubbles in me. What have they done to him? Bright green light begins to encase my body, but then I feel another presence. Is someone coming?

Turning toward the door, I wait. Time passes, and I slowly let out a breath I didn't realize I held. But that feeling of being watched can't be shaken.

"Brooklyn?"

Another light spark joins us in the room. *"Staten?"* I ask.

Someone tugs on my hand. I look down and see slender, light tendrils thread through mine. When I look up my arm, hazel orbs shine down at me. It's like both of us are made from pure energy. Neither of us have a solid form.

"It took me a while to hitch a ride on your magic and be brought with you to Bronx. I figured that you might need help locating him and figuring out how to reverse it."

"Thank you. You must be the one I felt enter the room."

He nods. *"Probably. I don't feel anyone else. But let's hurry just in case. They can't see us while we're connected in the bond."* He turns to his brother. *"Bronx, you look like shit, Bro."*

"I feel like shit, too."

"Try not to move. Play dead as long as you can. If you're being watched, your movements might give something away."

"What's next?" I ask.

"Let's try to pull on the connection and see if it'll retract enough to lead us back to our physical bodies," Staten says. *"Do you see the green light emitting from him?"* I nod. *"That's what we need to tug on. It's the end of the line connecting you, or I should say, us, to each other. While I don't have a bond directly with him, I do through you. I can't find him on my own, but with your help, we should be able to do this."*

I watch as Staten's phantom hand reaches for the green line that connects Bronx to me. He runs his fingers along it until his palm is pressed against my chest.

"Are you ready, Brooklyn?" Staten asks.

"Yes."

Staten's hand disappears, then his arm, and finally his body is absorbed into me. I see a pulse of light flickering down the line connecting Bronx and myself. That must be Staten. I think about how I got here, how it was dark and then turned to light. In my mind, I reverse it and try to imagine the lights turning off in a room.

"Have courage, Bronx," I say. *"Trust in me that this will work and we'll find you."*

"Always, Sweetheart."

"I'll be seeing you real soon."

Blackness covers my eyes and blankets over my feelings. It's cold and wet, just like Bronx said. Water drips in the distance. There's a zapping sound coming from the opposite direction of the water.

My energy ball meets with Staten's.

We burn brighter together.

Then we're flashed back into our human bodies. My eyes open, and I'm looking directly into Staten's face. A broad grin spreads, showing me his dimples.

"Do you know where he is?" Staten asks.

I pause and think about everything I know, of who took him and why. It doesn't make sense for him to be hauled off to some unknown place. It also doesn't seem likely that he's too far away from his captors.

"He's on the school property," I say. And without really knowing how I know that, I know it's true.

Staten nods. "That's where I think he is, too, under the school, in the tunnels. No one ever goes below the walking tunnels. But there is a sub-level farther below that connects to the old subway system."

"How do you know?"

"I know because it's my business to know everything about the school. While Manny and Bronx became instructors to learn the ins and outs of the Administration side, I hadn't always taught magic. In fact, I didn't really excel at any other class for that reason. I kept to myself a lot, like you did. So with that freedom, I scoured every inch of the property. I was the one who showed the guys the gate in the back of your dorm. It used to be covered with brush and the gate itself barely opened. Anyway, we got a snowstorm one year, and everyone was in the walking tunnels getting from class to class. I overheard a couple of instructors saying how crowded it was, and they should open up the lower level. That prompted me to look at the blue prints, and then I found out about the sub-tunnels."

"So you think that's where they are keeping him?"

"Makes sense. If there are tunnels, then there could be rooms down there, too. I'll take a trip to the city planning office again and see what else I find."

I check the time. "Be sure to be back by this evening's

meeting."

He crosses a fisted hand over his chest and nods. "Of course."

I walk Staten to his vehicle and wrap my arms around my body. He releases me and I wave. The scent of lemongrass fills my nose, and I know without turning around McQueen is behind me. His strong hands cover mine as I lean into him, pressing against his firm chest.

"How did training go?" he asks.

"Good. Staten is going to look something up that could help us locate Bronx. Well, we think we know where he is, but we need the layout to devise any kind of plan."

"If it's out there, he'll get it." We watch the taillights turn around a corner. "You should get some rest."

"I will later."

"This is the down time, while we wait for everyone else. You should at least lie down, and I'll tell you what my dad knows."

"Are you bribing me?"

"Yes, Babe, I am. We don't know what will happen tonight, and I'd hate for you to be exhausted while we rescue Bronx. We need you awake and alert."

That makes sense. I don't know when Manny, Declan, and Noelle will return. And Staten didn't know how long researching city records would take. I could rest for a while.

McQueen takes my hand, leading me back to my room. I hold on tight as I crawl into bed, dragging him with me. He kicks off his boots as he flips onto his back. We nestle under the covers, me on my side facing him.

"What did your dad have to say?" Maybe if I get him talking, he'll let me get back up. I'm not tired at all, being too amped up by thoughts of Bronx.

"I told him about Ireland, Sean, and Declan, who, by the way, can have the room he's in now. I'll be sharing with Staten again and when we get Bronx back, he and Manny will share a room." He runs circles over the back of my hand. "Dad asked why Noelle was here this morning, so I told him what she found out and why she, Manny, and Declan left. He said that he's heard the same rumors Sean has heard but doesn't have anything more definitive. While we were gone though, most of the dragons have been laying low. I guess meeting you really did placate them. For now. There are a few fringe ones still flying at night, but Dad has talked with a couple of them, so they are spreading the news of the drones and weapons being created."

"Good because when this is all over, I'll be having a meeting with the entire Pride, including the fringe folks." Then I decide to try something. I lower my mental barrier and connect with the Pride. *This is Brooklyn Bryer, your Pride Leader, and I command you to get your affairs in order.*

New York has been without a leader for too long, and I'm here to tell you that the position has been filled by me. I'm on an important mission right now, and after that, I'll be calling a meeting to discuss matters of living arrangements, the squabbling I'm hearing, and setting to rest the leadership. I've named Declan O'Dell my second and will formally introduce myself and him. Attendance is mandatory, by the way. Until you hear from me again, stay low and out of sight. The Academy is gunning for us. Be safe."

There are a few responses that wish me luck on my mission, to be careful, and to let them know the specific details of the meeting when I know them.

"You're laying the smack down on them? Us?"

"Yes. All of you need to be whipped into shape. I don't know how Regan ran things and don't really care. This is now my ship, and I will have order."

"Yes, Captain." He grins. "Call me your first mate. Or deck hand. Or even the scullery maid. I'll be whoever you want me to be."

I smile. "That has got to be one of the corniest lines I've heard in a long time."

"Did it work?"

"Are you trying to pick me up?"

"No. I thought we already addressed that. I can kiss you whenever now."

My cheeks redden. And he does just that.

His lips find mine. The kiss is urgent as if he's trying to make up for lost time from our few days of travel. His hands roam over my body, finally resting in my hair. He parts my lips with his tongue, searching every crevice inside my mouth, letting the tongue ring click against my teeth.

I do the same, gliding my tongue on his teeth. My arms tighten around his chest as my legs thread through his, pulling him closer to me. I nip his bottom lip. He growls. My dragon responds. She's pushing to the forefront. My magic blasts outward, causing the room to fill with green light. We both ignore it and continue our make out session.

McQueen's hands leave my head and roam under my shirt. My answer is to tug his T-shirt off. Eventually my own is removed.

We only break our kissing for a moment. I can't get enough of him. The bed dips as I roll on top of him. His fingers clench my sides, keeping me steady as I work my pants down my legs. I'm straddling him in only my undergarments, but I don't feel exposed around him. In fact, it's the opposite.

Our lips unlock, and I'm finally able to look down at him. He's beautiful. His body glows like mine, green and for the world to see. I unbutton his pants as he sits up and plays with a stray strand of my hair.

"You mean the world to me, Brooklyn," he says. "There

isn't anything I wouldn't do or give you. All you have to do is ask it of me."

I nod, knowing exactly where this is going. And I want it. I need him to be a part of me, part of the four of us that are already in my soul. This is right. It's what is meant to be.

At the same time, we both call our flames and press them into each other. My fourth and final protector is now carried inside of me—forever.

We seal our life bond with a kiss.

Chapter Thirty-Eight

My heart is literally full from bonding with all of my protectors. It's like everything that was missing in my life has been found through them. I can't imagine my life without them. Manny, Bronx, Staten, and now McQueen.

After our escapade in bed, I did fall asleep, so maybe I was tired. But now I'm wake and see jade eyes looking at me. McQueen smiles, and I return the gesture.

"You should get ready. Staten is back, and Manny just told me that they're headed here."

I stretch and nod. "Okay." I slide over him and get ready for the evening. Turning, I say, "Macklin?" He scowls. "I thought I would try it to see how it rolled off my tongue. It's kinda strange." He nods. "Thank you for bonding with me. Now, I'll have all of you with me in my heart."

It sounds really cheesy, but it's true. That's where I always find their sparks.

After a quick shower and change of clothes, I head upstairs and am greeted by Staten.

"Hi," he says.

"Hello to you, too," I say. He looks at me and then to his brother. Neither of us says anything, but he knows. He felt it. "What did you find out?"

"I figured I'd wait until Manny and Declan are here, so we don't have to go over it twice."

"Yeah, okay. Did you at least find something useful?"

"Yes."

We don't wait too long. The brothers chat as only they can. Then the doorbell rings. Staten lets the guests in. McQueen takes my hand and leads me to the couch to sit.

"Hiya, guys," Noelle says, and she saunters into the room, Declan close behind her. "We've got so much to tell you." She plops down into the love seat, pulling Declan, too. "My contact came through."

Declan scowls at her. She swats his arm. "We got the info, didn't we?"

"Yes, but I don't think you needed to do what you did," Declan says.

"Don't judge. We needed the information, and it was the only way we could get it in time."

I watch their discussion and can tell that Declan is not happy about something, but Noelle doesn't seem to think what she did was bad. I'll have to ask her about the details when we're away from the rest of the boys.

"Trust me, Brooklyn," Manny says. *"You don't want to*

know."

"*Yes, I do. If you need to tell me that through our mental connection, then it must be bad.*"

"*It's not as bad as you think. Declan is blowing it out of proportion.*"

"Okay," I say. "What did you find out?"

"Drop it, Decs," Noelle says. *Decs?* "Once we got to the school, I looked for Jake," she continues. "He's the one who's been feeding me the info."

"Among other things," Declan grumbles.

I look at him and then to Noelle, nodding for her to continue. "He said that they are moving to phase two with the drones. They are now equipped with tranq darts that are coated in titanium and have a lethal dose of ricin, which injects upon contact."

That sounds bad. "What do we know about ricin?" I ask no one in particular.

Staten moves away from the wall he was leaning against. "It can be a deadly poison. It's made from castor beans. If injected, it makes the body's muscles and nodes around the site swollen and painful. As the poison works its way outward, organ failure and internal bleeding will cause the body to shut down and die. It can be treatable, if caught in time."

"How?"

"There isn't an antidote, but getting the dart out of the

body as quick as possible, flushing out the spot with water, and cutting away the clothes near the infected area should help. If it's really bad, then intravenous fluids or eating charcoal may do the trick."

"Well, hopefully it doesn't ever come to that with any of us."

We're quiet for a moment. I don't know about them, but I'm thinking how terrible it would be to die that way, for anyone to have that kind of death.

Staten clears his throat. "I went to the city planner office and found the old blueprints of the school," he says. "And then I pulled out the transportation systems. We all know about the walking tunnels that connect the buildings on campus, but did you also know there is another level below that? It's an old subway system that was never finished. There are large tunnels and rooms down there that have been forgotten." He pulls out a large sheet of paper and lays it on the coffee table. Then overlays a second piece on the first. "When Brooklyn and I used her life bond to locate Bronx, I hitched a ride on that, since she and I are life bonded."

I take a quick glance at Noelle. She catches my eyes and smiles.

"While I didn't feel exactly what they are doing to Bronx, I can still talk with him in my mind and with Brooklyn. Combining our magic, we were then able to reverse the connection, and we both agree that he's being kept under the school, which is what prompted me to go looking again for these specs. I knew of both sets of tunnels." He points to the first map. "I think Allister is holding Bronx here, in this room. It's an interior room away from the main tunnel. It's small and looks to be a storage or supply closet."

"All right," I say. "Staten, I want you and McQueen to go over logistics on how best to enter, how to get to Bronx, alternate escape routes, and all that stuff. Get a list together of supplies we're going to need and start getting them. After you discuss it, let us know the plan of action." I turn to Noelle and Declan. "What else did you find out about the facility itself?"

She readjusts her body position. It doesn't go unnoticed by me that she scooted closer to Declan. "Jake was saying that the data is being stored on campus, too. It's in the Journalism building. They put it in there so as not to call too much attention. They already have the computers and tons of students roam that building at all hours of the day, gathering news information from around the world."

"We're going to need some jump drives, so we can download everything they have," Declan says.

"Yeah, I agree," McQueen says as he lifts his head from the maps. "I have some in my room."

"Actually, maybe we could download the information

and upload a virus to them. We don't want them to actually use the data, right?" I shake my head. "We need to corrupt their plans. If they don't have any data, they can't analyze it and move to any other phases. I'll need to get working on setting a trap for that." All eyes land on Declan. "What? I'm good at that sort of thing."

McQueen nods. "After this, I'll help you. Two are better than one. Staten can tell everyone else the plan for the rescue."

I turn back to Noelle.

"The weapons facility is actually under the Arts and Crafts Beer Parlor," she says.

"The one across the street from campus?" Manny asks.

"Yes. Jake said that it's the perfect front. It's closed during the day, and that's when manufacturing happens. Most of the work is automated, so only a couple of people need to be there to make sure everything is running correctly. If anyone comes in asking about anything, the people are instructed to say they're doing inventory."

"Smart."

"Yeah. Then at night when more people are around, the upstairs blares music and with the normal bar noise happening, that's when tests are conducted at the facility. No one is the wiser."

"Staten?" I ask. He glances at me. "Can I see that blueprint of the school? Does it have the Beer Parlor on it?"

He looks down and nods, pointing to the building in question. It's right next to the dental building and Warren Hall Coffee Bar. Blowing it up might not be the solution after all, with Warren Hall so close.

"Any ideas?" I ask. "Too many casualties if we blow it up."

"If everything's automated like Jake says," Declan says, sneering when he says that guy's name. "Then if we take the computer chips or rewrite some code, it should halt production. I won't know anything specific until we're in there, and I see what's going on. But destroying the computers won't do it alone. They'll just buy new ones. It has to be in the programming to either make faulty weapons or stop them from being made. It'll be a patch job until I see what they are using. Perhaps some of the materials could be tampered with or rerouted to another buyer."

Hmm. Declan's pretty good at this sabotage thing. Sean did say his son was good at tech stuff. He's going to be a valuable asset if he can do what he says at the facility.

So the question is: rescue Bronx or destroy the facility first? There isn't really a choice. Bronx always comes first. He's been waiting too long as it is.

"Hang on Bronx, we're formulating a plan."

Chapter Thirty-Nine

I don't have to make that decision. It's made for me when Noelle receives an incoming text on her school-issued phone. We hear her cell *ping* the recognizable sound and watch her read the message as her face turns white.

"What's wrong?" I ask. "Who is that?"

"Noelle?" Declan says. He gently takes the phone from her hands and reads the message and then shows me.

York Academy: Pass this message to Brooklyn Bryer.

You know who we have and are willing to make a trade. You for him. I know you guys are together or at least have been seen around campus. So I assume he means something to you. Since you outed yourself as a dragon, it's you we want. Not him. He's nothing to me. So take the high ground and save his life with yours. If not, then not only will he be the first blood on your hands, but more will follow. I can get to those you love. Parents.

Noelle. Bronx's friends. The list goes on and on. You for him. You have 4 hours to comply.

"That's it." I slam my hands on the coffee table. "Allister just showed his cards. We knew he wanted to back out of the truce, and we knew that he wanted me and not Bronx. But now he's threatening Bronx's life. We need to rescue him first then destroy the weapons facility. We'll need a plan." I look to Staten. "So what have you got for us?" McQueen and Declan rise and walk out of the room. I suppose to start planning on the tech aspect for tonight. It goes without saying that this is going to be fast, and time is of the essence. "We'll catch you guys up when we lock down the details."

Staten checks the time. "I know, Brooklyn, you'll want to go as soon as possible. And some parts of the plan will have to be modified since I don't know if anything has changed down in the sub-tunnels. While these prints show everything is open, there might be some tunnels that are closed. And the room I think Bronx is in, he might not be there. So we'll have to be flexible. McQueen and I wrote a list of equipment that should be in the garage." He turns to Manny. "Can you go grab all this stuff? Find a bag to put it all in."

"I should have a backpack or something." Manny leaves to pack the supplies.

"I think this is the best entrance." Staten points to a place on the map. "There isn't a lot of school traffic here, plus it's near a building that's primarily used in the daytime. We slip inside, descend into the lower levels, find Bronx, and leave. Yes, on the surface, it seems simple. But we must be ready for anything once we're down there. The halls are narrow, so we'll need to stay in human form."

This is probably one of the few times I'm thankful that Bronx and McQueen have pushed me so hard with training. Would Allister assume that we'd try to rescue Bronx? I would guess so. This is a trap, and we're going to walk right into it.

"As soon as we have Bronx," I say. "Depending on what his condition is, we might as well also have a look around the info center. Get the layout and any ideas. Thinking of the worst case, we'll be in our fighting gear and a bloody mess. Not appropriate for a night out on the town or even going into the journalism building."

"I agree," Staten says. "Bronx should be our first priority. We could send some of the younger dragons to the center to scout it out for us first. Dad can get them to go."

"Let's see how tonight goes first. I don't want to endanger anyone else if it's not necessary." I stand. "Okay, let's get ready for this evening."

Noelle gets up from the loveseat. "I hope you know that

I'm coming with you tonight. I might not be a dragon, but I know how to fight. And another set of eyes can help."

While I don't want to see my best friend get injured or killed, I know she won't be swayed. Once she puts her mind to something, there is no changing it. Besides, she wants to help rescue her friend, too. And maybe a little of it is getting revenge on Sax's death by stomping over Allister's plans. Who am I to stop her?

"Did you bring extra clothes or weapons?" I ask.

She smiles. "Um, we sort of took a bunch out of the school's arsenal before we left. I snuck the boys into the girls' weapon room and we cleared house."

"Have I told you how much I love you?"

"Not today." She winks. "I know I'm the best. That's why I'm your bestie." She takes my arm and leads us toward the stairs. "We'll be getting ready for tonight. Later boys."

Both of us change into our fighting attire. Then we head out into the garage and grab any weapons we can carry or strap onto ourselves. We look like we are headed into a war zone. I guess we are. Noelle told me that she had the same suspicions I had about this being a trap, and she's glad I'm letting her help us get Bronx back.

By the time I grab the last of the daggers that gets strapped into my custom boots, the boys are dressed in all black. Swords are draped across their backs, guns are in holsters on their hips, and I'm sure knives are hidden in compartments on their bodies. They had all that in their rooms? Manny's trunk is still open, as the boys take the remaining weapons, extra cartridges, and ammo.

"Ready?" I ask. "Let's go."

I don't confirm that McQueen and Declan have everything they need. They would have told me if they needed more time. We pile into two vehicles since we can't all fit into one, especially because Bronx will be with us on the way back.

Noelle rides with me, Declan sits next to her in the back seat, and McQueen drives us in his mom's Mercedes Benz, the same vehicle we took to Sax's funeral. Staten drives in his SUV with Manny riding shotgun. Our vehicle follows them through the city. We've all turned off our cell phones in case we are being tracked.

Besides, me and my boys can communicate with our mental abilities. I'll have Noelle and Declan stay close to one of us.

Declan.

"Hey." I turn my body to face the back seat. "Since you're my second now, we should be able to speak with each other through our minds. You're one of us. Sorry I didn't think about it before."

"Yeah, okay," he says. "How does that work?"

"I don't know. Let me ask Staten. Hold on."

"Staten? How do I let Declan into my mind but not allow him access to you guys at the same time?"

"It's all done via magic. If you only want him to speak with you, then that's all you need to think about."

"Okay. Sounds simple enough."

I bring my flame into my palm, giving only a small part of myself. None of the pieces from my boys are infused with it. It's a tiny, greenish ball.

"Declan," I say. "Hold out your hand."

I transfer it into his waiting palm. He stares at it for a bit, then clenches his fist, and absorbs the magic into himself.

"Can you hear me now?"

"Yes, Brooklyn. This will come in handy tonight and when we storm the facility."

"I only gave you access to me. If the boys want to allow you into their minds, they'll have to do it. But now that we're all connected, one of us has to be with Noelle at all times."

"Don't worry about her. I've got that one covered."

I nod. He doesn't need to tell me anything about their relationship, if there is one.

"Stop having a full-on convo without me," Noelle says. "I know you're talking about me and my safety. Declan will protect me, and I promise I'll do what anyone tells me to do. I know my limitations and can't go up against magic users."

"I'm sorry, Noelle." I reach back and pat her knee.

"It's all right. It's not your fault I don't have any magic or that I'm not a dragon. I'll use other attributes if necessary."

During the rest of the ride, I'm antsy. My leg keeps bouncing against the seat. Then my fingers twist, just how my stomach feels. It's not until McQueen squeezes my hands that I stop. Calming magic floods into the spot where he's touching me. My leg stops moving. A tingling sensation travels up my thigh and spreads everywhere in my body.

Before my brain can let the rest of my body know what's going on, my stomach cramps and I topple over.

"Brooklyn! What's wrong?" McQueen asks.

"It's Bronx. They're doing something to him. He … he's trying to block me from his pain, but that seeped through."

"Hold on, Bronx. Just a bit longer. We're almost at the school."

The familiar wrought iron gates of York Academy loom ahead of us. The rest of the campus is quiet, even from the college students. We park a block off the main entrance and walk the rest of the way. We stay close to buildings and hide as much in the shadows as we can.

Circling back to Broadway, we enter into the Arts Building. No one is around this time of the night. I expected a few students would still be practicing, but all is quiet. Perhaps too quiet.

Only a few hallway lights illuminate our way to the basement. Manny digs into his backpack and doles out flashlights. We save our magic for later. In hushed steps, we descend the stairs into the walking tunnels.

Staten leads the way, checking the map that he keeps rolled in his back pocket. "Should be just up ahead," he whispers.

No one says anything as we creep along. Noelle is sandwiched in the middle of the group, McQueen taking the rear. We make a couple of turns and then find a locked door. Staten uses a bit of magic to open it and waves us forward.

Inside is a rickety, old staircase. It doesn't look like it's going to hold much of anything, let alone one of the guys. We proceed with caution. It's dark, and I can't see the bottom. I could use magic and send it to my eyes, but I conserve that in case it's needed later. Manny opens his pack once again and finds a glow stick. He cracks it and tosses it down the stairwell.

Staten pokes his head down to scan the area. "It's all clear. After this, we'll be in the lower tunnels." He pulls out the map. We huddle around. "We're here," he says, pointing, "and this is where we're headed." The room is maybe a couple of blocks northeast from where we are standing. It looks to be underneath the Teacher's College. "There are a couple of ways to get there, but I don't want us to break up. We go as one. Follow me and keep watch. Once we're down there, no more talking. Use our mental connection if you must communicate."

"Brooklyn?" Manny asks. "Can you feel him? Are we headed in the right direction?"

I stop walking and let the group pass me. Manny comes to my side. Closing my eyes, I zero in on the part of myself that's Bronx. I feel a slight phantom pain on my cheek. Was he hit there? The light that connects us zooms outward. I can see it with my mind's eye. Using that, I open my real eyes and walk where it leads. I veer off into another tunnel.

"Staten," Manny calls. "Hold up."

"Turn around, guys," I say. *"Bronx is this way."*

Now, I'm leading the group of rescuers without a map. But I know how to get where we need to be.

Chapter Forty

The closer we get to him, the greater the pull. After taking a few wrong turns and meeting a dead end, I finally hold up my hand, signaling everyone to stop. I push magic into my ears and listen. Tilting my head, a banging sounds floats back to us.

"Is that him?" Staten asks.

I nod. *"Be careful, everyone."*

We slink down the dark hallway, flattening against the sides. So far, this mission has been uneventful, but it can't last long. *Way to jinx it, Brooklyn.* No sooner than I think that, we turn the corner and stop.

Up ahead are Level Three students. They haven't spotted us yet. We creep backwards and back down an empty hall. I don't know how many there are, but what I did manage to see was four doors, two on each end of the tunnel.

"He's in there," I say. *"Probably behind one of those doors."*

"It didn't look like they were guarding it," McQueen says. "More likely they don't know who is being kept behind the doors."

"If they knew, someone might have let him out. He was an instructor."

"Yeah, which is why I think the students don't know," Staten says. "If they drugged him while the Threes are milling about, Bronx would stay quiet, so whatever they are doing down here, they can go about their business."

"We have to get behind those doors."

"I know. We need a distraction."

"What are you guys saying?" Noelle asks as she walks toward the front of the group.

"There are four doors up ahead but there are students there."

"Then that's my cue. Did anyone get a look at the kids? Maybe I know some of them. Since we've all been sorta grouped together, I know most of the school now."

We shake our heads. It was too quick of a look. I don't even know how many Level Threes there are in the hall.

"Maybe Jake is around and if he's not, someone will know him. He might have said something to them about me, and I could say I'm looking for him. That he told me about the place."

"I don't like it," Declan says.

"You don't have to, but it's a good idea. Even if he's not

down here, I could still go looking around and come back and report what I find."

"I don't know, Noelle," I say. "It's dangerous. Allister knows you're my friend. If he's here too and sees you, he might put two and two together and assume that I came. He sent you the text which brought us here."

"It's a chance I'm willing to take. We need to know which door Bronx is behind."

I sigh. It's a plan. Not great since we're putting her in a boat load of potential danger, but it could work, too. "It's up to you, Noelle. You know what we're up against and what's at stake."

"All right. I'll go, then. Wish me luck." She hugs me and takes a couple of steps down the hall. An arm snakes out and grabs her, spinning her body back toward us.

"Not so fast," Declan says. "Just in case I don't see you for a while."

My boys and I back up to give them some space. I drag McQueen along, so we can give them as much privacy as taking two steps away can provide. Every word is still heard.

"I know we haven't known each other very long," he continues. "And I know you recently lost someone important to you. I don't want to rush you into anything you're not ready for, especially for a serious relationship or anything. But before you walk into the snakes' den, I need you to know that I'll be waiting for you on the other side."

"Ah, Decs."

That's all I need to know about them. They lower their voices to finish the conversation. They do seem to care for each other, and I'd be glad to see my number two and best friend together. But that's down the road. Now's not the time for thinking of that, only of Bronx. He needs us.

"Hey guys?" Noelle says. "I'll be back as soon as I can."

We nod. We're another step closer to having Bronx back with us where he belongs.

Declan takes Noelle's hand. "Be safe."

I can tell he really doesn't want to let her go. Their joined fingers slowly part as she takes another step.

"Hey, wait up," I say. I can't believe I'm going to suggest this. I lean into Declan's ear. "Why don't you go with her? You can tell me what's happening through our connection. That way if you need us, we can be there in a flash."

"I'll say he's a family friend visiting abroad," Noelle says. "No one would think anything different since he has an accent. And that'll keep my cover about Jake, too."

"We can figure that out as we go." Declan nods to me, then leads Noelle back the way we came and into the line of fire. He immediately opens the connection through our bond.

"I'll keep her safe, Brooklyn."

"You better."

I'm left with an antsy McQueen, a stern Staten, and a calm Manny. As McQueen paces back and forth in the short hallway, Staten pulls out the map again to study it. Manny leans against the wall with his eyes closed. I know he's ready for anything, even though he seems to be resting. By the bunching of his muscles, he's anything but calm.

"We're just entering the main tunnel," Declan says. *"There are about a dozen people up ahead. I can see the two doors on the left side."* I relay to the boys what my number two has said. *"No one is paying attention to us. Noelle is going to try the first door."* My body is tense, anticipating what's behind the door. All I know is that Bronx is somewhere down here, and he needs us. *"He's not here. Just a bunch of spare parts and junk. We're heading back out to the hall and will get to the second door."*

Manny squeezes my hand.

"All right, second door ..." There's a pause in Declan's voice. *"Shit! Someone's coming. We're just closing the door and stepping back into the hallway. Hold on."*

"What's happening, Brooklyn?" Staten asks.

Of course, he can feel my anxiety. "As they got out of the first room, someone's stopped them."

"It's okay. They'll be okay."

As soothing as the words are, it doesn't lessen what I feel. This was a bad idea.

"Okay, false alarm. We're good to go. Noelle said that she's looking for Jake. The guy just said that he's here somewhere. Now, we're making our way to the third door."

"Everyone's fine. Noelle just asked if Jake was there."

We wait with baited breath; there are only three doors left to check. McQueen stops his pacing and stands next to me.

"Let me take a quick peek inside the second room. I didn't get a chance to before we were interrupted." A few seconds tick by, and then Declan is speaking again. *"They have a dragon in here. He's tied up, bound, and has a muzzle on. Not sure if he's dead. Let me go check."*

"Be careful. If he's one of mine, he won't know you're my second and now part of the New York Pride."

"In the second room, they found a dragon," I say.

"We need to rescue him, too," Manny says.

"I know. If he can't change back to human form, we'll have to come back for him. Our first priority is getting Bronx."

"He seems to be okay. I think he can smell that I'm a dragon, or he's too weak to fight. The room is much too small for him to be here. He looks uncomfortable. Maybe a couple legs are broken. His tail might be, too. How should we handle this?"

"As much as I hate to say it, leave him there and continue on to find Bronx. We'll come back for him."

"Okay, we're walking down the hall to the other end. It'll be a

couple more seconds as long as no one stops us. Ok. We're inside the third room. Ah …"

"What is it Declan? What do you see?"

"It's a torture chamber. Manacles hang from the wall. There's a table in the center. Looks like blood."

My hands clench. I don't need to tell the guys that information. Perhaps they expect it, but if they know for sure, they'll charge in there. That'll definitely blow our covert operation.

"Bronx isn't here, either. But the blood, it's fresh. Maybe we just missed them." Seems about correct if my phantom pain was just when we descended into the tunnels. Did they know we were coming, so they moved him? *"We have a problem."*

"What is it now?"

"Noelle is talking to someone. Someone named Chris. You know him?"

"Yes, he's our friend."

"They ran into Chris," I say.

"That could be good," Staten says.

"He's asking her where she's been. That she can't be down here, but she asked why he was. Mr. Astor has all the magic users in Level Twos working on this stuff and word is that Noelle is possibly helping you. Everyone is looking for you, and they are to bring you in by any means necessary. Deadly force if it comes to that. But Chris doesn't seem to want to take Noelle in. Hmm,

we're being ushered into the fourth room now by Chris."

"What's happening, Declan?"

"Noelle asked Chris if he knew where Bronx was being held. Chris said that as a favor to her and you he'll lead us there, but that's all he can do about it. He says he's sorry. Okay, we're in the fourth room. It's a bunch of couches, tables, chairs, and a small fridge. Looks like a breakroom of sorts."

"Now what?" I turn to my guys, "Chris is helping them. He's going to take them to Bronx."

"Chris is checking the door. He's motioning us to follow. Should we? Do you trust him, Brooklyn?"

"Yes. He's had ample time to shout and get others to assist. And he's our friend. I was just with him the other weekend at my cabin. But stay alert, just in case."

"Will do."

I scrub my face with my hands.

This waiting is going to kill me, if Allister doesn't first.

Chapter Forty-One

I double over with shooting pain in my leg. It's as if someone took a cattle prod to it, turning the electrical feed to high and let me flounder like a fish. What are they doing to him? My body doesn't know it's not real. I lay convulsing on the floor.

"Brooklyn!" Manny says in a hushed whisper. "Bite down on this." He hands me the strap from his backpack. "Stay as quiet as you can. Remember, no one can know we're here."

The wracking and twitching stops, and I slowly nod. I gasp, and my body finally relaxes. "I'm okay," I grit out. "It's not really me. They're doing something terrible to Bronx."

"They'll find him," Staten says, close to my ear.

"Or we'll go charging in and level this place," McQueen says.

"Declan?"

"Yeah, sorry. We've been walking in the tunnels for a mile

already. Chris said a few more to go. If you guys follow us, be careful. There are students all over down here, and they all have a picture of you on their school-issued phone. They are to apprehend you by any means necessary. Chris led us down the main tunnel, so you guys might be able to find an offshoot and follow that way. He doesn't know how long Bronx will be here, so Allister must not have told the students the end game."

"As soon as you think you know where he is, let me know, and we'll move closer to you. We can't be miles apart for a rescue."

"I know."

I pull the map from Staten's back pocket, so I can find the direction my friends are headed. I lead them away from the main tunnel, back to where we came from. We'll be able to speak louder without so many students around. Once I deem we're far enough away, I trail my finger along the path where I think Declan told me. Everyone around watches.

"If they are headed over this way." Staten points. "Then he could be in the maintenance garage where they keep the broken cars. Or if they go here, there is an office used as the control station. Worst case is if they continue the way they're going, they'll wind up even lower and into the sewer system."

Gah. Please don't be in the sewers.

"I can't stand here much longer and not do anything. Declan said that they were headed down this way." I repoint to the map. "If we take this tunnel, we'd be in place to quickly go to either room. If things goes sideways, we'll be there in a flash to help Noelle."

"Okay," Staten says. "Let's start walking. We'll take the long way around. Manny and I are recognizable. No one will know McQueen, but people may assume that he's one of us. Strike first, ask questions later." He waves us forward. "Remember, stealth mode."

Why did he look at me when he said that?

No one speaks while we walk the few miles. No students cross our paths. The only sounds made are echoes coming from adjacent tunnels and the lone *drip, drip* coming ahead of us. It's been a while since I've felt any phantom pain from Bronx. Perhaps they've stopped torturing him.

"Bronx?" I ask. *"If you can hear me, we're almost to you. We've sent Noelle and Declan ahead of us. The plan was for her to ask for her contact, but they ran into Chris instead, and he's leading them to you."* Since I haven't heard from my number two in a while, I check in with him. *"Declan, we've been walking toward you guys so we're closer. Any update?"*

"I think we're headed to the area where they used to fix the cars. Apparently, there are a few vacant ones. Chris says we're almost there—correction, we're here. Noelle and I are hidden in a stairwell while Chris goes ahead and scouts how many people are there and if Bronx is here or in another garage farther down.

So just a second while we wait for Chris's return."

I tell my boys what Declan has said as we jog toward the tunnel that will lead us to the maintenance shops.

"How far out are you guys?"

"Why?

"You guys need to hurry up and get to us. Bronx is here, but he doesn't look good. I can't carry him by myself, and if we get ambushed, that leaves Noelle defending all of us."

"We're on our way." I nod like he can see me. "We need to haul ass to Declan. He's found Bronx and needs help carrying him out. Let's move." We run the rest of the way, not caring if our footsteps are loud. Bronx has been found. Now, we need to grab him and get the hell out of dodge. As we sprint down the last hall, we hear whispers ahead.

"Declan? Is that you we hear?"

"Yes. We're trying to wake your friend. He's passed out cold."

The door to the garage is wide open. Bronx's bruised body hangs from rusty chains just inside a subway car. Chris and Declan are trying to lift him to untie his red wrists from the ceiling restraints. "Bronx!" I yell as we run into the room. "Hurry, get him down."

"Oh, god, how could anyone do this to someone?" Chris asks.

Bronx's brothers are by him in a flash, assisting.

I scout the room for any hidden doors, rooms, or people milling about. Seeing Bronx's broken body hanging, I doubt that Noelle or Chris had the mindset to secure the room.

"This is Allister's doing," I say as I rejoin the group. "Is this what you guys are fighting for? Look at him!"

"Brooklyn?" Chris swings his head in my direction. "You can't be here. Mr. Astor has everyone looking for you."

"I know. But we needed to rescue Bronx. So here I am."

"Yeah, Noelle has told me as much. Look, I don't know what's going on and why you're on the run, but I'll do what I can to help you. We're friends."

"There is something much bigger going on than what Mr. Astor is telling the students," Staten says. "We can't get into it here. We need to get Bronx out."

McQueen and Manny carry Bronx between them. Bronx does not look well at all. He's not conscious. His face is swollen as if someone used it as a punching bag, one of his feet sits at an awkward angle, and blood drips from the corner of his mouth.

"The quickest way is to turn left the way we came in," Chris says. "Take the staircase at the end, continue up past the walking tunnels. Keep climbing until you hit the sewer cover. You'll come out on Manhattan Avenue, near Hancock Park."

As soon as we head out the garage door, footsteps sound down the hall. Brian stops short from slamming into us.

"What's going on—" He glances between me, Bronx, and Chris. "Brooklyn? Chris? Is that Bronx? What happened to him?"

"Long story that we don't have time to explain," I say. "We need to get Bronx to the hospital to get checked out."

"I was just showing them the way out," Chris says.

Brian got the same message as the rest of the Academy: bring me in. Indecision flares across his face for a split second. Then Brian steps aside to let us pass. "I'm sorry, I didn't know," he says. "I heard voices in here, and I already called for backup. Brooklyn, I didn't know it was you, otherwise I wouldn't have called."

"How long?" I ask.

"A minute, maybe more. It was my shift to guard Bronx. I stepped away for a couple of minutes to relieve myself."

"You knew about this, dude?" Chris asks. "Why didn't you say anything to me about it?" He hits his friend in the chest. "We're roommates and it's Bronx! We had him for a Skills Instructor."

"I know, but Mr. Astor said this was a top-secret mission, and he said that Bronx is a traitor to the slayers."

The boys continue to haul Bronx's broken body down the hall; they didn't stop to listen to Brian's excuses.

"How much farther, Chris?" I ask.

"It's just up ahead." He points to a door that we would've missed if we were by ourselves.

"You guys go," Brian says. "I'll distract them."

I shove my boys through the door and grab Noelle's hand. Declan pushes her in front of him.

Loud footfalls come from behind us. They're running. Then shouts are heard.

"Hey, guys," Brian says. "False alarm. It's just my buddy Chris visiting me. No need for the rest of you to come in here." A door slides shut.

"Hi," Chris says. "Came to see what Brian was up to."

We scramble up the metal stairs. McQueen heaves Bronx's body over his shoulder and climbs the steps. As soon as he's at the top, Manny takes him while Staten pries the sewer cover off that leads into the walking tunnels.

Flashes of lights bounce off the walls, encouraging us to move faster. Noelle is almost to the top of the stairs. I'm right behind her when a head pokes up the stairwell. Our eyes meet. It's not someone I recognize.

"Stop!" a guy shouts at us. "How did you guys get down here?"

"Oh, um, we took a wrong turn back there and just found the exit," I say. "We're needed up top now."

All of us hang on the rungs. Staten doesn't stop lifting the cover off. He climbs the rest of the way out and then reaches back for Bronx. Manny heaves him up and then follows suit.

McQueen waves Noelle to go ahead of him but then

blocks Declan. "We need to help Brooklyn," he says to him. "If they come up here, we need to get her to safety."

Declan nods as he freezes on the steps.

"Was that our prisoner?" A Level Three guy asks as he looks at us.

"No," McQueen shouts down. "Just a buddy of ours who twisted his foot not watching where he was going, so we helped him up."

Glancing my way, the first guy says, "Hey, you look familiar. Do I know you?"

"No, I don't think so." I motion for the boys to continue to climb. "Maybe you've seen me around campus. I just got here to the school, so I'm still learning my way around the tunnels."

"Yeah, it does take a bit of time to figure out which way goes where."

A third head comes into view. This one I recognize. "If they're needed up top, just let them go," Brian says. "We need to get back."

"Yeah, okay. Don't get lost once you get into the walking tunnels."

I smile. That was close. Too close. McQueen motions Declan to continue past him and then holds out his hand to me. I gladly accept as he lifts me up the final few feet. We let a communal sigh out. We almost got caught.

But we have Bronx.

Chapter Forty-Two

Declan is covering the hole with the sewer cover when we hear, "They're escaping!"

That gets us moving as the grate slams into place. We don't wait to see if they're following us up the stairwell. Staten and Declan drag Bronx between them as Manny takes the rear, sandwiching Noelle and myself in the middle of the group. We run as best we can down the walkway tunnel, hoping that we don't pass by any students. From behind us, the grill scrapes open as a dozen York students climb out of the hole and step into the walking tunnels.

Boroughs.

I know none of the slayers, and Chris and Brian aren't with them. They either have been captured as traitors or possibly are distracting more of our pursuers. I hope they're okay. They just helped save our asses. And they're my friends.

Bronx is leaned against the wall as the boys ready for a fight.

"Don't kill them," I shout. "Only injure them enough that they stay down."

We fan out and form a line, blocking the entire width of the hall. Noelle stays near Bronx, and Declan is right beside her. The pounding of shoes gets louder.

"Get ready," Staten says.

"Watch for the titanium bullets," Manny says. He must have seen guns, too.

The students don't recognize us, or their brainwashed minds override the fact that here before them are instructors from the school. They carry titanium shields. Some pull guns. They're going to be our priority. As far as I know, we can't stop a bullet.

"How are we going to defend against them?" I ask.

"The only thing we have is our magic," Staten says. "It'll slow the bullets, but we can still die from them. So watch out."

"We need a plan or something!"

"The only one we have is for you to change into your dragon. While a few bullets won't kill you, if they all unload on you, it could. But you'll be stronger in your animal form. All of us won't fit down there anyway. And they only know you as a dragon, not us."

Can I do this? They are my pride, my responsibility to

keep safe. As humans, they'll never survive the gunfire. And Bronx is still out of it. Noelle doesn't have any magic. That seals my choice. I must do this.

Calling my magic to me, I change my body into the dragon, transforming in a matter of seconds. It's the fastest I've ever done it. This is an emergency, not some training exercise. It's my boys' lives at stake. My friends' lives.

"Get behind me," I say. *"I'll try to take out as many of the students carrying the guns as possible."*

Thankfully, the ceilings in the walking tunnels are so high that I think I'll fit and still be able to move around.

The slayers come around the corner and skid to a stop after seeing a twenty-foot green dragon standing in front of them, black smoke billowing from my nostrils.

I still have a good few feet until the top of my head touches the ceiling, and have a bit of room to maneuver on the sides. I lumber forward and knock a few of them with my head. Others I take out with my tail all the while the Level Threes are firing their weapons. A few hit my body as most bounce off my scales.

My boys are right behind me. I can feel their presence. The students I've pushed to the ground fight against my boys. I don't take the time to watch over them. They can take care of themselves.

Continuing forward, I disarm as many of the slayers as possible. More are filing up from the manhole. I need to stop any more coming up. I shuffle toward the hole and blow dark smoke. It fills the halls of the lower levels. Then I spot Chris and Brian. I watch as their eyes dart at me and then move behind me. They look at each other, then back at me again.

I think they've made the connection as to why Allister wanted me so badly, and why Bronx was the bait. Secrets are being spilled out. I can only hope they side with me.

Brian raises his harpoon. Instead of throwing it into the fray, he dismantles the rope. He hits the nearest kid over the head and watches as he falls to the ground.

Chris glances at him for a split second and then runs into the fight. We pick the slayers off one by one. The students don't know whom to trust. Chris takes his weapon and decks the nearest fighter. She goes down.

I blow a fire stream high above their heads. Everyone flattens onto their stomachs. Screams fill the tunnel, along with more smoke.

The *pop* from gunfire rings. More are hitting me, breaking through the scales. I'll have some bruises on my chest and on my back where the wings sprout from.

I don't stop, still using my tail as my primary weapon against the slayers. Between Brian and Chris, they've managed to disarm half a dozen students. Brian ties them up with his rope. I don't know how we'll restrain the rest of them, though.

A few more students get past me. My boys will take care of them. They are the second line of defense.

All around I can hear guns, swords, and grunts, and it's all echoing off the walls, leaving me a bit disoriented. With my enhanced hearing, I can't really tell where the sounds are coming from.

The haze prohibits some of my vision, so I don't notice until it's too late a gang of slayers approaching me. They all have guns out and pointed in my direction. They're too close for me to use my tail. I could head butt them, but then my face will be in their line of fire. Staten said I could take a few bullets. I hope that means a dozen or so.

I brace myself for the pain. Shots fire. The first few I don't even notice. But then a sharp twinge on my lower throat and just under my wings sends searing pain rippling through me. I can't let them take me. I won't go down without a fight. If that means I have to kill them, then ... no, I'll think about that if and when it comes to that.

"Brooklyn!" Manny says. *"Stay focused and push through the pain. We can feel what you feel."*

For now, all I can do is keep standing and dodging their shots. With me being a huge target, the barrage continues. I hold my head higher to shield my eyes, leaving my chest exposed and vulnerable.

"How are you doing, Brooklyn?" Staten's voice faintly passes in my mind.

"I'm holding my own for now, but I don't think I'll be able to fend them off much longer."

"You don't have to," McQueen says. *"There are only a few left, thanks to your friends Chris and Brian."*

The ringing subsides, and I flap my wings to clear the smoke around us. I can finally see the damage. Most of the slayers are tied up or are lying on the ground, guarded by my boys. Manny and Declan are each favoring a leg, and Staten is caressing him arm. And Noelle is still standing near Bronx, protecting him as if her life depends on it. I owe her for keeping him safe. She does have a nasty cut across her face that will need to be looked at.

Chris holds his side, blood oozing between his fingers, and Brian's head has a large gash in it, along with a black eye. They both approach me.

"So," Brian says. "You're a dragon and that must be why Mr. Astor wants you so badly in exchange for Bronx. Now we get it. You're the reason the Council is up in arms, and there's a coup on the rise." I nod. "Brooklyn? You can understand me, right?"

I lower my head to their level. They take a step back.

"She won't hurt you," Noelle says. "It's still her. She knows who you are but just can't voice it." She comes to stand next to me. She's so short; she doesn't even come up to my chest. I carefully wrap a claw around her petite body and pull her closer to me. Rumbling starts in my throat. "I know, Brooklyn. I love you, too."

"She's a," Chris stutters. "A dragon? Has she been one all the time?"

"Kinda obviously, Chris. But she only just came into her powers recently, and she showed the Slayers Council. They agreed to live in peace. The Council granted them land. It's Mr. Astor who backed out on their deal with the dragons."

"What are we going to do with these guys?" Declan asks. "We can't leave them here, nor can we bring them with us."

"There's a storage closet near here," Brian says. "We can lock them in there, and later we'll send someone to get them."

"Okay," Staten says. "Let's get moving before more people show up."

"You guys go ahead," I say. *"I'll transform back, so I can walk down the halls better and climb the stairs to get to the ground floor."*

I push Noelle away from me and start the shifting process back into my human body. My magic flows out and blankets the tunnel in a soft green light. My protectors are already walking the prisoners toward the end of the hall, where Brian says there should be a room. I catch a couple of them glimpsing my way since they're curious about me being a dragon. And this is the first time they've witnessed anyone changing.

No one was killed today. A few are badly hurt; we'll need to find a first aid kit.

Up ahead a door opens, and the York students are shoved inside. We don't find any medical supplies. As soon as we make it up top, we'll let someone know where they are.

I'm back in my body, my leather pants and duster jacket firmly in place. I catch up to Noelle and lean against her. I'm exhausted. My legs take two more steps, and then I'm falling face first into the gray cement.

"Brooklyn!" Noelle shouts.

My vision goes black.

Chapter Forty-Three

I'm on the ground when I wake, staring into five sets of eyes. Something runs down my face. Is that blood I feel?

"Don't try to move," Noelle says. "You've been shot and took too many bullets." She presses my shoulders down. "One of the boys will have to carry you until you can get patched up by a doctor. Staten gave you as much magic as he could to stave off you bleeding to death or having the titanium kill you."

"Thank you." I reach for his fingers, then send any magic I can muster to heal myself ... which isn't as much as I'd like.

He nods. "Manny, you take Brooklyn. Declan and McQueen take Bronx. I'll be in the lead in case we run into anything. Chris and Brian, take the rear, and think of a plausible excuse why you're with us."

"You guys are with us, right? I ask. Manny steps to my side, squats, and carefully lifts my frail body into his arms.

"After what you just witnessed, are you changing sides?"

"Look, Brooklyn," Brian says as he touches my shoulder. Manny and the boys stop. "We haven't really been friends for all that long, but you're a Level Two. You're part of our class. Everyone got to know you better as Kill Shot, and the few of us who hung out at your cabin ... well, I'd like to think that we are your friends. I, for one, can't turn my back on that. You've done nothing bad to me. Sure, you turn into a dragon—which, by the way, is super cool—you're still Brooklyn. The shy, loner girl who I've come to like hanging around."

"Yeah," Chris chimes in. "Friends don't let friends die just because you're a dragon, and Mr. Astor says we should hunt you. He didn't tell us key information. Granted, we never asked, but still. I think if many of the students know about you and what you are, they'll side with us, too."

"How can you go against centuries of knowledge and your upbringing," I say. "We've all been conditioned to kill the dragons. What's changed?"

"I can't speak for everyone else," Chris says. "I think part of it was getting the opportunity to kill something. I know I got caught up with the thrill of it. But now that I know you and what you are ... it's different, somehow. Perhaps both sides have erred and should have started talks a long time ago."

"That's Allister's fault. He never wanted peace. He kept

the Academy thriving and getting more students to enroll. We think he's been lying to the Council about numbers and objectives."

"So yeah," Brian says. "Maybe we should have asked questions and not follow blindly. Or raised our hands more during class to question how things are. I for one didn't think to do that. Like you've said, we've been conditioned all of our lives to hate the dragons and kill them. But seeing you be one and transform back into your human body ... like Chris said, it's different now that we know you." He turns to my boys. "I'm assuming you guys are dragons, too?"

None of them confirm the question. Instead they start walking down the tunnel.

Could that be possible? If we do get the Slayers on our side—my side—could we win this battle without any more bloodshed? Allister wouldn't have an army to do his bidding. He'd have no warriors on the field. Then my dream I had of us versus them wouldn't come true.

Staten holds up his arm, stopping everyone. The boys flatten against the walls. *"What's wrong?"* I ask him.

"There's someone up ahead. I can smell him."

"Should we go back and use a different tunnel?"

"No. Let's just wait here and see what happens. It could be a college kid."

McQueen and Declan lean Bronx against the wall,

resting their own shoulders. I really wish he'd come to, so we know he's okay.

"Bronx, please wake up. You just have to be okay. I love you."

Staten gestures for us to proceed.

We climb the metal stairs leading to the ground level and should come out near Hancock Park. Staten is the first through and surveys the area. He sends a bit of magic up to surround the manhole as we all ascend onto the sidewalk. Chris is the last one up as Brian closes the lid.

"Why, thank you, boys, for delivering the exchange." Allister stands a few feet away and steps out of the bushes. *Is that true? Have they betrayed us?* "I didn't think you would, but here you are, bringing me another dragon and returning our prisoner."

"How did you know?" I ask, squirming out of Manny's hold. He gingerly sets me on my feet. I can't look weak in front of Allister. Well, any weaker than I already do.

"Ah, you forgot about the school-issued phones." Allister taps the side of his head. "I heard the distress call that Brian made and then enabled the GPS trackers on all students."

Boroughs.

"I watched the group of them move fast and thought they were on to something," Allister continues. "So I waited to figure out where they went. Then they remained in the same area for a while, and I assumed that they ran into something. Eventually, some moved while others didn't. Guessing it was a fight down there, and they met up with you."

"You can't fight us all. There are more of us than you."

"Is that so?" Allister steps forward. Not enough to close the distance, but to show us that there are people behind him, hiding in the shadows and in the shrubs. "I brought back up."

Double boroughs.

"Chris and Brian, step away from these traitors and fall into line."

Neither one of them move. They look at me, then to Mr. Astor.

"No," Brian finally says. "You lied to us, all of the students. You told us that the dragons were bad, savages, when in fact, they aren't."

"And you know that because you met *one* of them?"

"One is all I need to know," Chris says. "She's one of us. A dragon, but nonetheless."

"So be it. You'll die with them then." Allister turns his head to the people behind him. "They've made their choice. Try to keep her alive, but it's not necessary. We already have one, but two would be better since she's a female, and we could learn a lot from that."

We are out maneuvered, out gunned, and with two of us out of commission, our odds aren't great. But I won't go down without fighting for what I know to be true. And I know my boys will be at my side.

The park floods with magic from both of our sides.

The shrubbery parts as I count dozens of students, staff, and council members.

"Don't hold back," Staten says. "They won't."

McQueen lays Bronx on the sidewalk. A small moan escapes Bronx's lips. Is he finally coming to? God, I hope so. Declan comes to my side, Staten on the other. We brandish our weapons and crouch. We will not be the first to strike. I won't go back on my word. This is on the slayers, not the dragons.

"We won't hold out very long against twenty skilled fighters," I say. *"Since everyone knows what I am, I might as well fight in dragon form."*

Manny squeezes my shoulder to let me know he agrees.

Drawing on the magic that's already in the air, my body quickly shifts back into the multi-colored dragon as my protectors step aside and allow me to change. The transformation isn't as fast as it was earlier. I've lost a lot of blood and energy. All the slayers shuffle back as I land on my front feet. I know a magical protective barrier surrounds us, and I let out an earth shattering battle cry.

Allister waves everyone forward to charge. The others follow his lead.

This is it. This is our final stand.

Let it be known I'm here and will fight for my pride.

Wait. That's it.

I unlock the wall that I've constructed in my mind blocking out all of the dragons in my pride. They can help me. Us.

Chapter Forty Four

"*This is Brooklyn Bryer, your Pride Leader, and I call on you now. I'm on the ground with five other New York dragons and we're outnumbered, but we will fight against the slayers. Defend me. Defend your Pride. Defend your brothers. Come to Hancock Park and be the dragons you are.*"

My mind tingles, as my Pride answers.

"*I'll come.*"

"*I'm on my way.*"

"*I'll be there.*"

Everyone is locked into a fight. Actually, we all are battling against two, if not, three people. Unlike the tactic I used in the subway tunnels, I don't hold back. Fire blasts from me at the few fighters before me. Trees burn and grass smokes, clouding the area. My massive tail sweeps back, knocking over a few unsuspecting slayers.

"*To your left,*" I tell Staten. He leaps to his right, missing the line of fire I send his way.

"*Thanks!*" he says.

Turning my attention to McQueen and his opponents, I say, *"Duck right now."* He does, immediately throwing himself to the ground. Where his head was minutes ago, my claw slashes the open air, swiping at four slayers.

We continue using our mental bonds until I hear the dragons' cries from above. They made it. Slayers look to the sky as dozens of colored dragons descend into the area. My boys and I don't even glance their way; we can feel their presence.

A volley of arrows sails into the sky as the dragons dodge them as best they can. Some stick, but it doesn't stop or slow them from landing. We continue to fight as more magic is poured into the area, creating a larger barrier. With this many dragons in the park, the buildings around us are going to be leveled.

Now, this is the war we are meant to fight.

The slayers, led by Allister, continue to drive us back. The adults are precise with their strikes from years of practice. The younger ones still hold their positions. In groups of threes and fours, they gang up on the dragons. Multiple weapons with arrows are brought forth, something very similar to the ones from my dreams.

Allister sashays to the side, pulling something from his leather vest. It looks like some kind of device. It's too quick for me to get a good glimpse of it before it's placed back into his pocket.

My attention is brought back to the slayers before me. I can't get trapped with them. Harpoons and javelins fly all around us. And then a barrage of arrows slam into my wings, side, and tail.

I'm fighting the ropes off. Using the fire building in my throat, I roar, letting everything around me burn. My body thrashes around, but I'm still weak from the titanium bullets from earlier. I can't shake off some of the lines falling across my back. The adult slayers make quick work, and I find myself caught. A snarl escapes from my lips.

"I'm stuck," I call out to anyone who can hear me. No one answers; they're all too busy battling against their own slayer and not getting caught.

Then I hear whirring sounds from the sky. Blinking dots come closer. Are those …? Boroughs! The drones. That must be what Allister was doing with that doohickey thing in his pocket.

Lasers scan the area and find their marks. Deadly tipped arrows rain accurately, lodging into the bodies of the dragons. The slayers just turned the tide of the battle, and it's not good for us.

The ground shakes from the large animals falling from the sky. The slayers make quick work and capture them as they land. I watch as more of my Pride are dragged and tethered under titanium nets and ropes.

I twist and turn and still can't untangle myself from the

precarious situation. And then I don't have to. A black form slinks its way toward me. Someone is army crawling on the ground. Then I see a finger sliding up to his mouth.

"I'm here, Brooklyn," Bronx says. "Sorry it took me so long. I just needed a bit of time to recuperate and gain strength."

"Oh, Bronx. I don't care. I could just kiss you right now."

"Save that for later. I think I owe you much more than a few kisses. Here, hold still, while I cut the lines. It's not looking good for us, Sweetheart."

"I know. What are we going to do?"

"We need to take those drones down and those specialized weapons. We don't stand a chance against them all. And I don't think we'll be able to stay in human form for much longer." He looks to where his brothers are still trying to fight.

It's not good for them as I follow his line of vision. Staten's magic is almost depleted. McQueen and Manny are still favoring their legs that were injured from our first fight below ground. And Declan? He's barely standing and trying to protect Noelle, who seems to be holding her own.

"Hey, our prisoners!" a staff person yells.

"Hurry, Bronx!" I say. "Staten, Manny, McQueen. You guys will be able to withstand blows and fight back better in your dragon bodies. Each of you must decide for yourself if you want to reveal yourselves in front of the Slayers Council. I will support whatever you decide."

"I'll be able to protect you better in my dragon form, so I'm *doing it."* Bronx continues cutting the ropes as he talks with his brothers. *"Guys, I'm over getting Brooklyn out of a jam. I'm going to shift into my dragon form, and we're going to try and take out the drones."*

"We're shifting, too," the boys say as one.

A few more seconds later, the last of the lines are cut and I'm free. Then I'm staring at an olive-green dragon breathing fire toward the slayers. Bronx's shift was lightning fast. We take to the sky. The screams and the pointing from the fighters don't go unheard with my enhanced hearing. I look back to the ground as three more green dragons fly toward us. Flames spews from their mouths, destroying everything in their path to get to us.

We fly in a formation; I take the lead. Staten and Bronx flank my sides. I quickly glance down at the ground to make sure that Noelle is still okay. Declan is near her, both kicking some major ass. Sean must have really drilled fighting skills, more so than York does.

The drones are ahead of us, blinking their locations as if they are beacons telling me exactly where they are. Now, we just need to figure how to take them out of the sky.

"Any ideas?" I ask.

"Dragon fire!" Staten says.

"Worth a try," Bronx says. *"Let's circle around spread out a bit, so we're not flying so close and being one gigantic target in the sky."*

We each hone in on a drone and blast if with flame. They fly backwards and out of the line of fire. They're quick and nimble, and our tactic isn't working.

"We're going to have to leave them and get to the ground and help where we can. Dragon fire does nothing against their titanium exteriors."

They nod, and we swoop toward the ground, taking out as many slayers as possible. Something in the corner of my eye catches my attention. The manhole cover we came out of is moving. York students rise out of it, led by Madi. Her telltale, curly red hair blows in the wind.

Brian runs toward her. I hope he's convincing them to be on our side. A few more dragons go down by the time we land. With all five us, the ground shakes from our body weight.

We don't have time to think about them; we have adult slayers descending upon us. The drones hover, scanning for the dragons, so their arrows can release.

Chaos ensues as students now flood the park, taking their weapons against the adults. Yes! We still need to do something about the drones, though.

Allister.

He's the key.

Chapter Forty-Five

I really don't want to kill anyone, but Allister must be removed from his position at the school, as head of the Council, and the leader here in this battle. Plus, we need that controller from in his pocket to deactivate all the drones.

Being in dragon form, I won't be able to get close enough to him. For an older guy, his moves are lithe. I need to be the same. My skills are severely lacking if I go up against him alone. There's no way I'd be able to overcome him.

I land and shift my body back to human. I have no other alternative. As a dragon, I don't have any fingers and I need that device.

"What are you doing?" Manny asks.

"I need to stop Allister. He has a remote in his pocket that I think controls the drones. I'm too big as a dragon, so we're going to have to fight him one on one."

"You will do no such thing," Bronx says. *"That's what we're*

here for." His body changes into his human form as he lands next to me. *"Besides, he and I have a score to settle."*

"The rest of you guys, help out where you can. And be careful."

My protectors glide and swoop and dart between the fighting. It's difficult to see if we're winning or not because there are so many people in the small area. Many of whom, I don't know. But what I can assume is all of the adults in the area are not on the dragons' side.

I spot Allister in the far corner, opposite where Bronx and I landed. "Let's go," I tell him as we make our way through the park, battling slayers as we pass. We try not to linger too long as the head of York Academy is our primary target. "Are you okay to do this? I mean, I'm grateful and all, but you've been tortured for days and—"

"I'm strong enough for this. My wounds are healing. Any magic I can spare I'm using to fix myself."

We stop and help Chris, who is locked against a pair of slayers. Now with three against two, it's easy to take them down.

"Hey Brooklyn, not sure if you saw Madi or not, but she cleared out the tunnels and brought everyone with her," Chris says once our fight is done. "I managed to tell her the shortened version, and most of us are with you. We don't have the same expertise as the adults, but there are more of us than them. We are holding our own, but I don't think we'll last much longer if something doesn't change. And soon."

"Already on it. We were on our way to Allister to stop the drones, but saw that you needed help. We could use some more cover if you can provide it."

"Sure thing."

I scan the park and notice that many bodies litter the ground. Maybe only a dozen dragons are standing. Many of my Pride are caught under nets. More are still being targeted from the sky by the drones. Chris is right. We won't last another five minutes.

"Hurry!" I yell.

Chris and Bronx part the sea of bodies and slayers for me. We stop only when necessary to assist a fellow fighter. Then I'm standing in front of Allister.

"It's over," I say. "I don't want to kill you, but I will if I have to."

"Oh, it's not finished yet," Allister says. "If you look, you don't have hardly anyone left. In a few more minutes, you'll be overrun, and then we'll rid the world of your kind."

"You don't have to kill him, Brooklyn," Bronx says. *"I'll do it for you."* Addressing Allister, he says, "You and I have some unfinished business. You kidnapped me, tortured me, left me starving, all for what? You thought I'd turn Brooklyn over to you? Our bond goes deeper than what

your puny mind can fathom." Bronx swings a fist in Allister's direction.

He easily ducks. "You won't win this." Allister's body shimmers as he calls his magic. I've never seen anything like it. It's bright yellow, more potent than he let on during the Council meeting the other week. Bronx doesn't stand a chance against that.

"Staten!" I scream through our bond. *"I need to draw on your magic."*

"Take what you need, but I don't have much left."

"It'll have to be enough."

Tapping into what little Staten has, as well as anything I can siphon from my other boys, I pull it deep inside of myself. I gather the full strength of my own green flames. I hold Bronx back. Then I unleash my power against Allister.

His magic bashes against mine, a battle of wills.

Then I take a tiny piece of magic from my other Pride members and harness it, sending it through to beat Allister back. He's more experienced, but I have will and determination on my side.

Allister's hands thrust toward me, and I fall on my butt. The force of it knocks my magic from my grasp. Bronx and Chris are right next to me, ready to defend me with daggers and swords. Allister draws something from his inner pocket. I think it's the drone controller, but this is shiny, not black.

The barrel of a gun is pointed at me. Allister swishes his hand with his magic still in full force and blasts both Chris and Bronx to the side. He cocks the safety off. I scuttle backwards and bump against something. I'm trapped.

I grab my flames again.

This is it. We've lost. My Pride will carry on without me. How many dragons has he captured and plans to do experiments on? Boroughs, I can't let that happen.

Using the last of my magic, I send it rocketing out of me, blasting everything in its path. Like a bubble bursting, it smashes and levels the trees, people, and blows away the discarded weapons that dot the ground. But Allister is still standing, gun aimed at my chest. He casually brushed my magic away from him as it soared passed his body.

I've failed.

"I'm sorry, guys." I let that pass through the bond to my four protectors and Declan.

"BROOKLYN!" they all scream, including my second.

The gun goes off. The world slows down. I see the titanium bullet coming at me. From my left, I see Bronx flinging his body toward me. He's not going to make it.

The silver speck is nearing my heart.

Closer. Closer.

The tip breaks through the layer of my shirt.

I cringe, but the ground presses against my back leaving me no other place to go.

Then, suddenly, the bullet changes direction.

It leaves a red trail of blood across my chest.

I look where the burst of magic came from.

Noelle stands with her hands outward.

What? She doesn't have any magic. How is that possible?

Then Allister's body crashes toward mine, a red spot blooming on his chest. His hand goes to stop the bleeding, but his head hangs low as his knees buckle.

He lies in a pool of his own blood—dead.

"Noelle?" I ask. The world rights itself back to normal speed. "How?"

She looks at her hands as if they belong to someone else. "I don't know."

"We'll figure that out later. Right now, grab the remote from Allister's pocket."

She doesn't move, still staring at her upturned palms.

"I've got it," Bronx says. He kneels next to the body and flips it over. Open eyes gaze at the sky. "Got it." He fiddles with the switches, and we all look at the drones. They are still flying about, but after a few moments, they stop and drop to the ground.

"What happened?" Staten asks as he steps to us. The rest of the boys are shifting mid-land and hover over me. "Are you hurt?"

McQueen helps me sit up. "No, I'm fine. I don't know what happened," I say. "One minute I'm looking at the barrel and a bullet coming right for me, and the next minute, the bullet is moving in another direction."

"Did it hit you?" Manny asks, bringing me in for a hug as his hands roam over my back and head. I realize he's checking for injuries.

"I don't think so. I can't say for sure."

We hear footsteps approach as we tense, ready for battle once again. Just because Allister is dead, doesn't mean the fighting will cease.

"It's over," a voice says. I stand so I can get a better look at who's speaking. "You're safe now, and we won't let anything happen to you."

"Dad?" I ask. "Why are you ... how did ...?"

He grabs my shoulders hugs me. "We've been keeping tabs on Allister ever since you left the school. As you know, he tried kicking us and John off the Council, but we have many friends, and they'd tell us when the meetings were."

I step out from under his arm. "Is Mom here, too?"

I watch him look at his hand, empty his gun's chamber, and toss the weapon onto the ground. "Yes, she's around here someplace. John and Kennedy are probably with her."

"John and who?"

"Mrs. Mercer."

"How?"

"When Allister disappeared from the school, Kennedy followed him into the lower tunnels. She found the dragon and released him, by the way. He's safe for now, a bit bruised, but otherwise okay. And then when Allister went topside, she phoned me, and I let the others know where to meet up. We arrived here just as your Pride of dragons landed."

"Honey?" I turn my head at the sound of my name. "Are you okay?"

"Mom?" I run to into her open arms.

"Oh, thank God you're safe. I thought ... I saw Allister with the gun and couldn't get to you in time."

"I'm okay now." We walk back to our group. All the fighting has stopped.

John and Kennedy are corralling the few remaining adults who are still standing. They're gathering weapons and tossing them into a pile.

Brian and Madi are releasing the dragons caught under the nets. Chris is holding his head, resting on a bench. But then he slowly rises and helps his classmates free my Pride.

Holy boroughs. We did it. I saved them. My Pride.

Declan is consoling a stunned Noelle. I know she'll be okay. She can lean on him until she's ready for a relationship. And since he's my second, he'll be around for a very long time.

"With Allister gone," Dad says, "I'm assuming the interim head of the Slayers Council. We will work with the New York Pride for peace, land, and whatever else you need, Brooklyn."

I smile.

My protectors flank my sides.

We have survived.

My boys. My family. My friends.

Yes, we've lost many over the last few weeks and during the missions the slayers were sent on throughout the years. My heart will always mourn them.

I'll never forget my friends: Saxon, Reist, and Lexi. The previous dragon leader, Regan, and all the other dragons who have died.

Epilogue

Two months after the battle in Hancock Park.

Dad held his promise and took over the Slayers Council. By unanimous vote, he now sits at the head of the organization, along with being the President of York Academy until the school can be disbanded.

As his first official act, he terminated all programs that Allister had in production: drones equipped with tranq darts, the making of titanium bullets and arrows, and recalled all weapons from the slayers. It turned out to be kind of like a turn-in-a-gun program. Incentives also worked wonderfully.

The school he put on a one-year suspension. Training on weapons and the slaying of dragons changed to socialization sessions on diversity, living with multicultural difference, and classes like that.

I have a seat on their Council, as my dad also has one on

mine. We meet on a regular basis to discuss issues that arose over the weeks, lead times on new initiatives and programs, and, of course, the living arrangements for us.

During one of the last Slayers Council meetings, Dad brought out a map and dissected it into quadrants. The islands that McQueen had brought me to were part the dragon's lands. In fact, all of those islands and some in the Pacific Ocean along Alaska and California were also labeled as Dragon Islands.

We needed more, though.

Apparently when I called the Pride to fight, the couple dozen that answered weren't all of them. They had heeded Danzel's warning and mine and kept low, out of sight.

Shortly after Allister's demise, I called for my own Council meeting to formally introduce myself, Declan as my second, and my protectors.

We held it at the Queen's residence. About ninety dragons came. It was a nice and informal gathering. We decided to have a BBQ in the backyard, so they could mingle and chat without the pressures of being inside and in a boardroom.

They were able to meet me in my own element, relaxed and happy.

And boy I am ever.

I stayed with McQueen and his family since I needed to be involved with the daily activities in the dragons' lives. It just didn't make sense to stay with my parents at the townhouse. Danzel is a great leader, and I named him my primary advisor. He's patient and lets me decide things on my own.

Declan slipped into his role as my second in command. He's with me almost as much as my protectors. They still don't like it, but it is what it is. Declan actually is a wonderful second. Not only is he knowledgeable about technology, but he's extremely organized. He's been a god send to me, and I can feel that we'll become great friends.

He and Noelle have been seeing each other. Neither have put a title on it since it's still too soon after Sax's death. But I see that they both like each other, and there's something brewing between them. It'll either work or not. And it's none of my business. I just want to see them both happy, and if that ends up with each other, then great. But if not, they both know that they'll have to work something out. Noelle isn't going away, and neither is Declan.

For the short term, Staten moves into the bedroom with his brother, while Manny and Bronx share another room down the hall from mine. Declan stays with the Queens, too, until some more permanent living arrangements can be made. It doesn't seem to be that he's in a hurry about leaving, though.

Since I'm officially an adult in the eyes of the state of New York and am the Pride Leader, I need to stay within the borders of the city. But I want more freedom than the bustling city that never sleeps can provide. While I love the lights, Broadway shows, and restaurants, I can't help but think I need to set up headquarters someplace else and start fresh. Let it symbolize new beginnings.

As a graduation present from my parents, although technically I never graduated, they gave me the residence up north. The cabin my friends stayed at over my birthday weekend will always hold fond memories.

It's in the process of being remodeled. While I love most of the furnishings my mom picked out, it's still her style. Plus, some of the bedrooms needed to be gutted and turned into a receiving hall and the living room expanded to allow for a larger dining room.

The junior suite, which was always my room, is still mine. I decided to redecorate the master room and use that as the Council Room.

Each of my protectors has their own room. Oh yes, they will all live with me. They have earned their place in my heart and deserve to be at my side for however long our lives are. I hope it's a very long time.

And yes, Declan has a room there, too.

So it's the seven of us until the end.

We do everything together.

They are my family.

The End

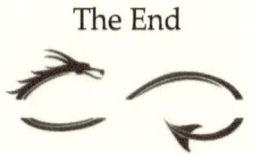

Dear Reader,

Like Urban Fantasy stories? Try out the Enlighten Series.

Zoe Jabril needs to devise a kick-ass plan to save the world ASAP. Otherwise, Armageddon starts the day she turns eighteen—and if that happens, everything is going to hell. Literally.

She could be any other 17-year-old attending parties and checking out cute guys—except she discovers her best friend is a Guardian Angel and the boy she crushes on is a Nephilim, both sent to protect her from the demons who want her dead.

Now Zoe has to deal with growing feelings toward the Nephilim, who spreads a strange electrical current through her body every time he touches her. And she's under constant attack from Demons, trying to stop her from fulfilling the Prophecy: a girl will be born who will unite Angels, Nephilim, Fairies and Werewolves to battle evil. Then she has to control newly found talents if she's to prevent the devil from escaping Hell.

SWORDS & STILETTOS: Book 1 in the Enlighten Series.

Acknowledgements

There are always so many people to thank. First and foremost is always the beta reader: Hilary. Thank you for speed reading this as fast as I was writing it.

To my wonderful development, Rebecca Jaycox. You know this story was also vastly different from my other books, yet you were confident in me that I could pull it off. And on such a fast pace. To Hilary, my copy editor for catching all of the missed commas!

Rebecca Norrine, you made such beautiful covers for me. I love them so much!! Thank you!!

Six Queens: Rhonda, Sarah, and Hilary … you girls are my rock!! You helped me keep focused, picked up my slack so I could do a rapid release with this story. Let's reign together!!

To the Six Queens ARC Team. Thank you for reading and reviewing in time for my release day!

To the Readers of Dragon Slayers. May you continue to love the stories I write.

Lastly, thank you to my wonderful hubby. Who I know doesn't fully understand all the book lingo. But bears with me until the end of the final product. Without your support, none of these stories would come to life.

USA TODAY bestseller, Amazon bestselling, and award-winning young adult author, Kristin D. Van Risseghem grew up in a small town along the Mississippi River. Currently, she lives in Minnesota with her husband and a Calico cat, named Daizy. Kristin also loves attending book clubs, going shopping, and hanging out with friends. She has come to realize that she absolutely has an addiction to purses and shoes. They are her weakness and probably has way too many of both.

In the summer months, Kristin can usually be found lounging on her boat, drinking an ice cold something. Being an avid reader of YA and Women's Literature stories, she still finds time to read a ton of books in-between writing. And in the winter months, her main goal is to stay warm from the Minnesota cold!

Kristin's books are published by Kasian Publishing LLC.